WIT

Katharine padded downstairs in a white terrycloth bathrobe; hair, uncombed; face, waking-up pale. Kevin Bryce had to repeat his first question twice.

"Sorry," she said. "Yes, I saw Evan the night I arrived."

"You went with him to his house?"

She seemed surprised. "Yes, I did."

"Did he return with you to the party?"

"No" she said.

"Did he offer to?"

She leaned toward the marble-topped coffee table and put sugar in her coffee. "No, he didn't offer."

Bryce gently persisted. "You didn't find that unusual?"

"May I ask if there's a particular reason for my being questioned on this account?"

"Yes. Evan's been dead since the night of the party. It appears you were the last to see him alive."

She was so still Bryce thought for a moment she might have gone into shock . . .

Other Avon Books by
Deborah Valentine

FINE DISTINCTIONS

UNORTHODOX METHODS

Deborah Valentine

AVON BOOKS NEW YORK

UNORTHODOX METHODS is an original publication of Avon Books. This work has never before appeared in book form in the U.S. This work is a novel. Any similarity to actual persons or events is purely coincidental.

AVON BOOKS
A division of
The Hearst Corporation
1350 Avenue of the Americas
New York, New York 10019

Published by arrangement with the author
Library of Congress Catalog Card Number: 91-91792
ISBN: 0-380-76286-2

First Avon Books Printing: September 1991

AVON TRADEMARK REG. U.S. PAT. OFF. AND IN OTHER COUNTRIES, MARCA REGISTRADA, HECHO EN U.S.A.

Printed in the U.S.A.

RA 10 9 8 7 6 5 4 3 2 1

To Teresa Chris, with many thanks to Michael

Author's note

I would like to acknowledge publicly the deputies at the Tahoe substation of the Placer County Sheriff's department for their kindness in assisting me with the research for this book. I would also like to make clear that all the characters and situations in this book are fictional. The Sheriff's department cannot be held responsible for any irregularities of procedure or bad behavior indulged in by the characters portrayed. The opinions expressed are also solely the invention of the author. I did, however, steal one or two of the department's jokes.

One

Shit!

It was rewarding to say the word out loud, to be vulgar in secret. It was dark and he'd stepped down too suddenly into a pothole on the uneven drive. His nostrils filled with the scent of dirt and pine. The air was cool but his skin felt hot, a prickly itch originating not from an external irritant, but from a fever within. Taking the flashlight from his pocket, he knew this rush of power and discovery was better than the sex he'd never experienced. He hurried forward, ready to enter not only a house but perhaps also a mind that, despite all reasonable efforts, had remained closed to him.

The doorknob turned easily and he smiled. With practiced and precise care he wiped his feet on the mat, adjusted his gloves, turned on the flashlight keeping the beam low. This cabin was fairly isolated, a chance passerby was an unlikely event, but he was naturally discreet—that was one of the qualities that had made him such a success—so he kept it dim enough that it might be mistaken for nothing more than an odd reflection of the moon's light on the window-glass.

The spareness of the room bored him. The leather on the wingback chair so worn he wondered why it hadn't been replaced, the rug before the fireplace ridiculous and gamey-smelling, the numerous books on the shelves cause for suspicion though he assumed them unread. There was little in the way of popular fiction, mostly classics and small books by obscure authors. Some unfamiliar feel to the room made him ill at ease and he moved up a set of uncomfortably narrow stairs to an equally sparse loft. He sat at the desk there, opening the top drawer. Pens, pencils, erasers, bullets. He took a few pieces of ammunition in hand, sat back and rubbed them like worry beads, scanning the walls with the flashlight. Not much hanging there. One painting near the desk was all and the beam rested on it only briefly. Nothing in the typewriter roller. He was going for a deep drawer when something clicked in the back of his mind. He stopped, shone the light on the painting once more, specifically on the lettering in the lower right-hand corner.

Marin.

He got up and stood next to it, heart racing, beam not quite so steady as a moment before. This was no print. What had this man done—saved his coffee-and-doughnuts money? Secrets. Surprises. It seemed everyone had them. Unconsciously he pocketed the bullets, then lifted the painting off the wall with the happy confidence of a man who had suddenly discovered his mission accomplished.

Outside he took a moment to watch the light glitter on the lake, study the pattern of the car headlamps rounding the water's edge on the road below. Without further ceremony he threw the painting in the car and drove away.

Two

Lake Tahoe is a large body of water set 6229 feet up in the Sierra Nevada Mountains dividing California and Nevada. From the south shore, the north shore cannot be seen, only a chain of mountain peaks, jagged as a child's drawing. From the west shore the east is solid but not definable—trees, homes, docks mesh into a grey-blue mass. The water is clear. It used to be clearer until pollution took its toll. But even so rocks thirty, forty feet below the surface appear to spiral dangerously close. Standing on the edge of a cliff there is the illusion a diver could fall just as he could in Acapulco and swim safely to shore once more. But this is mountain water and it is stunningly cold.

A small part of the north, most of the south, and all the east shores belong to Nevada and what isn't National Forest consists mainly of casinos and motels. Many of the homes are rentals—modulars, cheap imitations of Swiss chalets. But they hide their ugliness behind the trees, bask in the reflection of the lake's beauty, borrow glamor from celebrity guests. The tenants are transient, concerned only with gaming tables, for this is a place where sable is paired with polyester, Grand Marnier washed down with Coca-Cola.

The California shores are different. A large chunk of the west is National Forest, though there are homes tucked away in the most unlikely places: small, homely cabins, half a century old; large, expensive hidey-holes, owned both individually and corporately. Further up the crooked highway to the north, the homes cluster more thickly in the trees. Tahoe City itself is clean and quaint. And though one shopping center goes so far as to simulate a Scandinavian village most are modern yet rustic enough to blend into the scenery. As healthy California sunshine is exchanged for healthy California snow, shopkeepers change their signs from "Sun & Sport" to "Snow & Ski". Coffee shops are not as plentiful as gourmet delis and trendy restaurants. Exercise hard, eat well, look good—there is an almost puritan logic applied to recreation.

But move on past Carnelian Bay and Tahoe Vista to King's Beach and two blocks off the highway this picture is altered. In a neighborhood of Tahoe originals—hunters' cabins and vacation homes whose prime is past—a small barrio exists, populated by illegal aliens who provide the cheap labor for motels and Nevada casinos. Like the underprivileged everywhere these residents often live ten to a room and rely on various unorthodox methods to make ends meet.

And it was here that Kevin Bryce, Sergeant at the Tahoe substation of the Placer County Sheriff's department, often resolved the crimes assigned to investigations—usually drugs and burglary. But before him sat a report on an oddity. No stero unit had been touched, no television or ski equipment—the usual fare—but valuable artwork. Affluent homes had been quietly broken into and paintings removed—not every week, not every month, not consistently enough to call in extra surveillance from Auburn, but enough to irritate the community.

In the office Bryce shared with three detectives he sat at his desk, having the choice of three views: one wall of bookshelves stocked with leatherbound copies of *Deering's California Codes*, the back of Detective Browning's hairless neck, or out the window to the velvet green meadow on the opposite side of the highway. Bryce stared at the meadow with an expression so serious it appeared angry. A top, a toy belonging to the captain's son, had found its way into the scales used for weighing in drugs. Bryce picked up the toy and absently fingered it.

The noteworthy point to Bryce in this particular burglary was not the burglary itself, but what had been stolen. This thief had always been predictable in his taste: landscapes, portraits, elaborate nudes. But catalogued before Bryce were a collection of names Bryce would have not thought his style: Kahlo, Marin, Dove.

So what did this mean? Had the thief experienced a broadening of taste? A change of market?

"Hey, I hear we got another one from Mister Class Act." A cheerful young deputy ready to do his shift on patrol strutted in, mouth first. "How about that? There's some wild rumor going around that he got into your place and took some expensive painting—name of a county, the guy who painted it."

Bryce saw the back of Browning's neck twitch as if he were dying to turn around.

"Mare-in. Not Marin," Bryce said, shaking his head and smiling.

The deputy whistled. "Boy, we have to sit down and talk finances. I need to know how you can manage to afford stuff like that on your salary."

So had the captain.

Bryce said, "No booze, no women, use firewood instead of PG&E."

The deputy laughed. "Shit, it's not worth it."

Still smiling, Bryce twisted the top and watched the pressure spin it around on the desk until it dropped right off the edge.

Three

Anticipation always whetted Jonathan Craig's appetite, so for breakfast that morning he consumed four extra-large buttermilk pancakes, three poached eggs, two orders of fried potatoes, corned beef hash and four slices of toast, washed down with strong coffee—though all this would do nothing to put meat on his thin bones. He didn't even pretend to read the newspaper and left it folded next to the sugar. He was too impatient to read and, besides, he knew all the local news. He shovelled down his last mouthful of eggs and sat back so the waitress could refill his cup.

A group of teenagers walked by and, spotting him through the restaurant window, smiled and waved. Jon gave them a friendly nod. He was something of a cult figure for the teenagers of Lake Tahoe's north shore, a position he'd earned by his friendliness, his sponsorship of community activities (particularly sports), his parties, and, most importantly, his ability to argue a point and win. He was a master in the use of words.

Most everyone thought he was wonderful; even those who knew he was not.

Jon's cousin Katharine was one of the few well-acquainted with the less wonderful side of his nature but that did not stop him from looking forward to her visit. It had been—what?—a year since he'd seen her? Of course, they talked sometimes on the phone. His bills read like a globe of the world: London, Majorca, Paris. But on the phone he found he missed the nuances of expression, the gestures that could be so revealing. Jon was sensitive to such things; his talent for reading them was what made him so successful in his job as family counselor.

He felt a hand on his shoulder.

"Seven tonight? Is that right Jon?"

It was Percy Metcalf, Captain of the Sheriff's department, a man who in profile gave the genteel appearance of the president of a small but distinguished college.

"Yes, yes." Jon smiled and pushed out a chair. He was careful to invite at least one member of the department to his social functions, for he was not without sympathy for their position in this small community. Money, recreation, drugs: it was a trinity that kept individual police from being invited to a lot of parties. Even dinner with the wife at the newest restaurant could pose a problem if the husband had busted the proprietor the week before. Also, Jon came from the school of the politically wise. Who knew when a police friend might be needed?

Percy sat and leaned forward. "Daughter's been doing much better since we've followed your advice," he said.

Jon smiled modestly. "You always have to use a firm hand with girls. Believe me, I know the problems." He idly opened the newspaper.

ANOTHER ART BURGLARY OF TAHOE RESIDENT

"Weekender this time," Jon said.

"Attorney from San Francisco. But you know them, Jon. I've got to tell you the men have really been enjoying the character doing these jobs, he's definitely a cut above our usual fare."

Jon cocked his head. "You haven't been getting too much pressure from some of the more conservative around here, have you? I doubt if everyone appreciates the uniqueness of this fellow."

"Well . . ." Percy frowned, as if he'd suddenly been caught enjoying himself too much. "He'll be caught one day, believe me. He'll push his luck."

"Yes. Of course. Make sure the men know they're welcome tonight. You all deserve a little fun."

* * *

Having finished his inquiries young deputy Martin Anderson stood on the veranda of a west-shore ski lodge talking to the owner, Petter Swenson. Petter was a tall, trim man; handsome in a strict military sort of way. His business was mainly real estate, though he appeared to spend most of his time overseeing the management of the lodge. He could be seen by the side of the road running there most mornings, a knapsack on his back. Anderson had been shocked and impressed to discover one day that the knapsack was full of rocks. Petter was in his late fifties, about the same age as Anderson's father had been when he died, and Anderson couldn't help contrasting Petter's good health and dignified manner to his father's own messy and alcoholic life. In Anderson's experience with Petter and his wife Inga, they had never failed to extend to him a genuine appreciation for the help he'd given them in his role as police officer. The attitude was not a common one, even among those to whom the police were obliged to offer assistance. Anderson found himself trying harder in order to live up to it, to feel he deserved this courtesy.

That was one of the reasons he was here this afternoon. On the advice of Sergeant Bryce he was following up on the burglary of some ski equipment. Normally this duty would fall to Bryce or one of his detectives, but they were occupied with the new art burglaries and he had been eager to take up the assignment. As a recent transfer from Los Angeles County he was determined to do well and he made sure his questions were both thorough and asked in a friendly and professional manner. The sergeant had been quick to impress on him the idea that all inquiries coming from the investigative division needed to be carried out politely and with attention to niceties, at least until necessity proved other means in order.

"It's probably going to be different here from what you're used to in LA," he had said. "It was different from what I was used to most of the time I worked San Mateo County. When I joined the Sheriff's department I was assigned to

East Palo Alto—that was before they got a police department of their own. My first night on the job we had three stabbings, two shootings and a rape. I was in Tahoe six months before we had a shooting here—and that was done by a frustrated deer-hunter who got drunk and shot the moosehead off the wall of a Tahoe City bar."

They had laughed but underneath the sergeant's kind scrutiny there was a sharpness Anderson hadn't missed. The message had been clear. Bryce expected a certain kind of conduct and, like all others in a position of authority, he'd be an asshole if he didn't get it. However pleasant he might appear now, however satisfying it might be to have his approval, he was not to be trusted.

"—the Craig party tonight. Will Inga and I see you there, Martin?" Petter was asking.

"No, sir, I'm on duty tonight," Anderson responded and could have kicked himself afterward. The sergeant had told him before that he used "sirs" where a name would be more appropriate. A little familiarity, Bryce said, wasn't likely to kill him—most of the time, anyway.

"Ah, Inga will be disappointed. But we will be having a party of our own later this month—for our wedding anniversary. Perhaps you will be able to attend that one." Petter possessed a severe, high-cheekboned face that he rarely softened by smiling, but he did so now.

Anderson smiled in return. "I'll do my best," he said.

Once back in his patrol car Anderson was disgusted to find his palms were sweaty.

Four

Katharine Craig was a tall woman, five feet eight and carried herself shoulders straight, stomach flat, chin slightly higher than it needed to be. Early that same evening she walked purposefully through the Lake Tahoe airport, a garment bag slung over her shoulder, a small suitcase in hand. In the airport's tiny parking lot she found, as she knew she would, an old '53 MGTD, British racing green. Taped to the steering wheel was a sheet of lined notepaper, folded once crisply through the center. Katharine ripped it from the wheel and found this handwritten message: *Here it is, as you requested. I hope this imported pile of junk breaks down on you. It's only right. That's what it does to me. Love, Jon.*

Katharine put the key in the ignition and slowly pressed the accelerator. Then, letting it up to the halfway point, she turned the key in one swift, decisive motion. The motor kicked over and purred.

Katharine burst out laughing.

But as she moved out onto the highway and took the west shore heading north, she felt a familiar tightness in her stomach. This was a road she knew well, she'd grown up traveling it. Her mother had died on it fifteen years before. And though Katharine had passed through here only a few times in the past ten years, her responses to its hairpin curves, the climbs and dips were instinctual, accurate. She didn't indulge in any of the conventional memories—happy or unhappy—of a homecoming. She concentrated on the road, the only situation over which she had control, and drove fast, often to the accompaniment of squealing rubber.

Half an hour later she pulled into the driveway of Jon's house and stared at it, vaguely amazed.

The place had started as a small stone house built by his father Samuel during the late '40s—a kitchen, a living room with an enormous fireplace, a loft with a couple of bedrooms. Twenty years later, having made a secure financial base in Napa Valley real estate, he had retired here. But in the years since Samuel had died and Jon had taken over the place had changed. Jon was an improver by nature. He improved people at work and when he was done with that, ordered improvements on the house. The simple stone structure was now surrounded—atriums, improbable turrets, and shingled huts sprouted off the sides like mushrooms on the grass.

Jon was at the door, his arms open wide. "There you are!"

"My God, you're here. I expected to wait for hours while you counseled an emergency mid-life crisis," she said, smiling.

"Actually, I escaped from a mother concerned about her son drawing phallic symbols on the grammar school walls. Quite well-drawn symbols, too. The boy could be quite an artist."

"Antisocial, is he?"

Jon shrugged. The open arms were reduced to a pat on the back, a brief kiss on the lips.

"He has a slightly screwy viewpoint of the world. It's typical of the artistic personality," he said sweetly.

Katharine, at twenty-eight years old, was a recognized sculptor. She glanced at her watch. She had been back exactly one minute. He's getting quicker all the time, she thought.

"Past your dinnertime?" he asked.

You could turn around, get in the car and in three hours be in San Francisco, she told herself. Instead, she linked her arm in his. "Way past."

* * *

Jon drove them in a four-wheel-drive Eagle station wagon, too new to have a license.

"Smells like the factory," she said, and other than "really" or "goodness" that was the last sentence she spoke. Jon filled her in on local gossip, mostly about people the last ten years had made distant. They parked in a marina parking lot. Between two shingled buildings the water, darkening to the deepest royal blue, was striped by a series of white masts; the sky rimmed the mountains with the last pale orange sunlight. The warm, early autumn temperature was dropping quickly.

"Remember the restaurant above the marina? It's getting better all the time," Jon told her.

When they were making their way around the building she asked, deliberately neutral, "How's James?"

"He's a lunatic. Just last week he got tipsy at a party and stole the firetruck out of the station. Then he ran into a tree and passed out. So he was, as they say, caught red-handed."

"Get the facts straight, Jon," said a voice from above. "I didn't pass out—I pretended to nap. I was doing research for my next book."

Jon snorted and James, seated on the railing of the deck above, grinned.

"You weren't hurt?" Katharine called up to him.

Jon answered for him. "No. He didn't *run* into the tree, he just *coasted* into it. Neither he nor the truck suffered any real damage." Jon appeared disappointed.

James came down the stairs, gathered Katharine in his arms, and twirled her around. He was a handsome man, over six feet tall, nicely muscled, if not overtly athletic, with thick, dark brown hair. His gray eyes had just hints of laughter lines at their corners. A successful novelist, he garnered not only critical acclaim but, with his last book, commercial success. He was only thirty-three. He gave Katharine an extra squeeze, then set her feet back on the ground.

"I have to give you credit, James. You do have a knack

for research,'' she laughed. Jon rolled his eyes and for a half second—no more than that—she was glad to be back.

''Katharine,'' James began in a rush, ''I don't suppose you know there's been a party arranged—''

Contentment slid into dismay. ''James, you know how I feel about parties—''

''Too late,'' he said, looking sad. ''You're already there.'' He held one finger in the air.

But Katharine wasn't looking at him. She was looking at Jon. He was smiling at some distant point on the lake. As if on his command, a breeze swept up, leaving Katharine cold. She put one foot in the direction of the car. James grabbed her hand.

''I don't like these things, either. And I don't have a date to help me through.''

Jon was already climbing the stairs.

She kept holding James' hand tightly as guests converged on them from every side. With composure she fielded questions:

''How are you—?''

''Where have you—?''

''Will you be staying—?''

And the new question to the roster:

''Is your alarm system in order?''

But she only let go of James' hand twice. Once when she greeted Inga and Petter Swenson; and again when she greeted James' brother Ed and his wife Laura. Her other hand held a glass of champagne which James signaled a waiter to keep filled. And Katharine, contrary to her usual habits, kept drinking. Somewhere around the middle of glass four she released him. The guests were dispersing to other corners of the restaurant. No longer quite the focal point of attention, she felt free to move through the crowd and take notice of her surroundings.

It was a small restaurant, closed to the public for the evening. Knotty pine walls were waxed shiny. Long tables covered in white linen with hurricane lamps for light were set in neat rows. A view of the lake was spread out for patrons by a series of connected windows. Lights on distant shores flickered in the dark; a breeze drifted through cool enough to send a white-jacketed busboy over to adjust the windows. The large bar (a place, Katharine assumed, where James spent a lot of time), carved with grapes and gargoyles, was well-stocked with exotically labeled bottles. A buffet in the center of the room provided roast beef, prawns, cheese, fruit, crudités. Katharine filled a small plate and took a seat.

A couple of places away was a man whose face was familiar, but whose name she couldn't remember. She was so bad with names, it embarrassed her. She thought he worked for the Sheriff's department. Irritating, she could remember that but blanked out on the name. He had a companion who looked very much like him; a younger, sleeker, shorter-haired version. Maybe they were brothers? Maybe she should just ask their names? Maybe she should move to the other side of the room? The younger one looked as if he expected her to make conversation. She'd had just enough champagne to leave her willing to make the effort. *Sergeant Bryce*, that was the older man. Thank God she could remember that much. A little more at ease she made some ordinary greeting and bit into a prawn.

"I've been fine," Bryce answered. "We haven't seen you around in a while. Have you been working on a commission?"

Anticipating a safe, uninspired exchange of small talk, she smiled.

"Yes. In France. And I took some time to enjoy the countryside with a few friends near Avignon."

The younger man leaned forward.

"I saw your *Ball-on-Chain* series in New York, not too long ago—"

Katharine hadn't realized until she'd eaten that prawn how hungry she was, how close to being drunk. *Damn you, James*, she thought. But it was an affectionate curse. She caught sight of Jon standing a few tables away, detained by a very short man Katharine knew instantly wasn't an American. Jon was watching her. The sigh that escaped Katharine was deep and discouraged, only partially stifled.

"—all those feet, all with ball and chain. It was interesting the way you—" The young man stopped, elongated in the shadows cast by the hurricane lamp, his face turned annoyed. "Of course, one wasn't quite sure what you *meant*."

"What I meant?"

"Yes, what was your intention? Were you only going for the obvious statement or did we miss something?"

Katharine's right eyebrow shot up. She positioned her fork carefully on the edge of her plate and pushed her chair away from the table.

"If you'll excuse me, I'd like another drink."

But Bryce reached across the table and picked up her glass. He set it down in front of his companion.

"Steve can get one for you," he said and smiled at Katharine, who would have made a protest if she hadn't been stopped by what seemed to be genuine apology in his expression. After a second of reluctance she relaxed back into the chair. (After some surprise and more obvious reluctance Steve got up to fetch her drink.) She tried to compose a social smile for the man next to her but knew she failed.

Bryce ventured kindly, "Steve is a very enthusiastic young man."

Katharine nodded and avoided direct eye contact with Bryce by watching his hands. Spread out over the white linen they were thick-knuckled, calloused, scarred. Distracting.

"Do you play the piano?" she asked.

He nodded, obviously surprised.

"Classical training?"

"Eleven years," he answered. "How did you know?"

Katharine bit her lip. His hands were the type more easily associated with chopping wood than playing music.

"It's the way your fingers curve—and you were tapping

out the base chords of the background music—you even had good fingering,'' she ended wryly.

He grinned and confessed, "I was a lousy musician. In high school I finally rebelled and signed up for wrestling.''

She looked at him and laughed. Then felt fingers on her shoulder and knew, without having to look, that it was Jon. There was always a possessiveness to Jon's touch, no matter how innocuously employed. Just as there was always a gentleness to James' touch, however much pressure was applied. There was never any confusing the two.

"Kevin's not boring you with detective stories, is he?''

"Haven't had the chance yet,'' Bryce answered.

Even in this inadequate light she saw something in Bryce's face that was at once amused and aggravated. She bent back to glance at Jon. He looked pleasant but his fingers, she was sure, if they stayed as they were, would bruise her skin.

Katharine pushed her plate away.

She managed to make her exit before young Steve returned with her drink. She slipped quietly through the party out onto the restaurant's deck, half expecting James to be there, remembering all the other times they had escaped from Jon's parties together. But the deck was empty and the air cooler than was comfortable, smelling strongly of pine. She took a deep breath, appreciating the scent, and tried to avoid thinking of how pointless this ritual visit had become.

"Katharine! There you are!''

The voice belonged to a small man, dressed in clothes too chic for Tahoe's social requirements. Evan Christie was the type of man other men loved to hate, that most women rather liked. Effusive, charming, and theatrical, even Katharine retained a fondness for his entertainment value though something about his nose, turned upward and out, made her think of a pig's snout. And his fingers, short and squat, reminded her of the nursery rhyme, "This little piggy went to market, this little piggy stayed home . . .'' He greeted her with an embrace both longer and warmer than necessary.

"You're freezing, girl. Look, you've got goosebumps," he said.

Moving out of reach, she answered, "Forgot to bring a sweater, Evan."

"Well, let's get you one. I've got a new house, Katharine. Right on the water, not five hundred feet away. Have your choice of any you like."

"Oh, no, really—"

"Come on," he coaxed. "I've got ulterior motives."

"You're flattering me, Evan."

"Yes, I am. *Intellectually*. I've got a new sculpture I want you to see. It's called *Three Doors in Life: Vocational, Political and Judicial*."

"Sounds heavy-duty." Inwardly, she winced.

"It's unique. Quite an *expression*," he told her seriously.

"It must be," she said, though she was inclined to be doubtful. But there was this eagerness to Evan. Slimy? Well, yes, he did have a gigolo quality. But he was so transparent, so easily dealt with, that Katharine was usually kind. She glanced at the restaurant. "Any sweater I want for my artistic opinion?"

"Scout's honor."

It was a decorative work for the sado-masochist. *Three Doors* consisted of three battered doors arranged in the manner of the three-way mirrors favored by clothing stores. Through the center door hundreds of spikes were hammered, sharpened tips set accusingly toward the observer. Attached to the left one were shards of glass, seven or eight inches in length, reflecting geometric patterns of blue light on the floor and ceiling. The third was wrapped from top to bottom in barbed wire.

"Well, what do you think?" The pride in Evan's voice was unmistakable. It might have been compared to the cackle of a hen who had just laid a prize egg.

Katharine took a deep breath. "It's quite a piece. Helluva lighting job."

"You see where we got the title?"

"We?"

"Yes. *Three Doors in Life: Vocational, Political and Judicial*," he began earnestly. "The glass door represents how so many are trapped by their jobs. All those high-rise glass structures, you see? The spiked door represents those imprisoned by the judicial system. The spikes, you see, represent bars." He gingerly touched the end of a spike with his finger. "The barbed wire represents political repression, *à la* Berlin wall."

She was silent for a time, thoughtful.

"What, exactly, do you want, Evan?"

"There's this woman, you see." He leaned close and Katharine could smell bourbon.

"And she did this sculpture."

Face flushed, he nodded. It occurred to her he'd probably had a lot to drink. From what she understood, he usually did. Getting paunchy these days, too.

"A closet artist. You'd like me to take a look at what else she's done."

"Yes." He seemed not only embarrassed, but also nervous, rolling on his toes slightly, occasionally throwing a fleeting glance over his shoulder.

"Sure. If you can catch me before I leave," she said.

"Katharine, you're a *doll*." Evan hugged her.

Moving away a step, she said, "Don't you find this a bit—I mean, it's not a friendly piece. I'd hate to lose my way in the middle of the night and run into it."

"To tell you the truth, I'm getting attached to it. I don't know why."

Katharine was sure she didn't either. Maybe he's in love with the woman, she thought. Must be nice.

"A little white wine, Kat. To celebrate."

She declined, reminding Evan about the sweater. While she picked a large black tweed from the designated closet, Evan padded to the kitchen, perhaps still intent on the idea of a little wine, preferably in his boudoir.

She pushed the thickly knitted cotton sleeves over her elbows, straightened the collar before a mirror where, in a white tank dress, she looked more attractive than she felt. Except her eyes, which were bloodshot, and burned. The day of traveling, the evening of socializing, left her drained. She shuffled out of the bedroom, turned left instead of right and wound up in the living room where she had to blink against Evan's splendid ultra-modern white-on-white style of decorating. *My God, this man has the most uncomfortable way of living*. Rubbing her eyes, she turned around and walked out of the room. She found the kitchen. Evan had a glass of wine in each hand.

"Sorry, love," she said. "I'm off to bed. *Mine*."

Surprisingly, he didn't argue. At the door he waved her a cheerful good-bye.

James was sitting on the steps of the deck. Katharine could see the crowd inside had thinned considerably.

"Escaped without my help this time," he said.

"You're not always around. I've had to learn to fend for myself." She smiled and sat next to him.

"Staying long?"

Not any longer than I have to, she thought. But she softened this before she spoke. "Probably not," was how it came out.

"Would you stay if I asked you to?"

She stared at him, surprised. But there was a neutrality in his profile Katharine found comforting.

"For how long?"

"I don't know," he said.

She paused. The lake looked like nothing but a great black hole. "I'll give it a week for starters."

"I'll teach you to sail. I've bought a new boat. A thirty-three-foot Hans Christian. I'm living on it now."

"Two weeks, then."

Though he was smiling, he didn't seem happy. She took his hand and kissed it quickly.

He said, "Another art burglary was discovered this evening. Kevin Bryce was called away. So was Jon. The people burglarized were clients of his, he's been counseling their teenager. The kid was pretty upset. So I guess with Jon gone I'm your ride home. Whenever you're ready."

"I'm ready." But still they sat, hand in hand. "You're not going to try to kiss me good-night, are you?"

He shook his head. "I'm going to take you into the woods and ravage your body."

"Thank God," she said.

Five

Kevin Bryce leaned against the trunk of a ponderosa pine, contemplating the lights of the house in front of him. It was an imposing place, built up against a steep hill, a four-storey hut on stilts. He saw the shadows of two of his detectives getting into their car, heard their shouts to the patrolmen, signifying the end of another unfruitful search of the crime scene. He restrained himself from digging his heel into the pine debri mounded beneath his feet. As part of this holding exercise he didn't turn when the sound of crackling twigs came behind him.

"Finding comfort in nature, Kevin?"

Bryce shifted, reflecting that Jon Craig was a congenial man. That, of course, was one of the reasons he was so popular with the lake matrons. Congenial and concerned. Always.

"Care for a cigarette?" Jon asked.

"Didn't think you smoked, Jon. Thought you didn't smoke, drank moderately and ate healthy food."

"I don't smoke," Jon told him, offering the pack. "But I keep a few cigarettes for those in need. It's supposed to have a calming effect on the nerves." Like a kindly tempter, Jon held the pack out a second longer before replacing it in his pocket. "When do you think it happened?"

"The Mathesons left September 20th and returned today, October 7th, so it must have been some time between now and then."

Jon laughed softly. "That's one thing I've always appreciated about you, Kevin. You're very succinct."

"Doesn't pay to talk too much, does it?"

"Doesn't it? I suppose not. It certainly didn't pay for the Mathesons. Or the Johnsons. Or the Sinclairs. Or the Cohens. Or the Talbotts—to name a few."

What was it in Jon's voice that made the back of his neck prickle?

Jon smiled. "They couldn't help talking about their new purchases, even discussed their alarm systems. Some of those things don't work well, do they? Always going off for no reason. Of course, there are others that are more efficient, present more of a challenge."

"I didn't have an alarm system. And I didn't talk about my painting, either," Bryce stated cautiously.

Jon answered quickly, excitedly. A soft breeze brought to Bryce a sour scent of nervous sweat. "Yes, you were a surprise. You see, I just scouted out your place to see what sort of person you were, do a final check. Your place is difficult to get to, it's no wonder you don't have an alarm. However, that little Marin on the wall was really unexpected." Jon didn't polish his nails against his jacket but so self-satisfied was his air Bryce could well imagine him doing so.

Bryce said, "You're telling me this because no one would believe it."

"Your Captain was at my party tonight. When Detective Browning's little girl came up with scoliosis I was the one who found the specialist in San Francisco. I have friends everywhere, Kevin." Jon checked his watch. "Oops, party should be over by now. I hate not to say good-bye."

Bryce crossed his arms and pressed his back against the tree.

"Doesn't make a good impression. You have to coddle people, you know. Of course you know. You're a policeman, you understand the social politics involved—especially in a community like this."

Bryce looked at him wonderingly.

"Jon, one of these days I'm going to nail your fucking ass against the wall."

In the dim glow from the house Jon's surprise was revealed, painfully contorted by the play of distant light.

" 'Fuck' is such a nasty word, Kevin. You shouldn't use it. Really."

Six

Four days after the fact and one day after the discovery, word leaked out that Evan Christie was dead; found decomposing as he hung on *Three Doors in Life*. The local women talked of his death sadly as they did their marketing, shopped in brightly decorated clothing boutiques, lay bikini-clad on the beach. The men spoke of it in considerably less sorrowful tones as they drank their morning coffee at their favorite counter, scrubbed the bottoms of their boats, or visited in the lobby of their bank. Bryce did not think anyone could sincerely say they were grieved, but all were affected by a degree of shock.

"Although frankly," someone told Bryce over coffee at the 7–11, "I always thought somebody's husband would get him."

Bryce had nodded. He had always thought so, too. But that was before he found the Mathesons' paintings locked in the basement of Evan's home.

It was a singularly uncommon way to die. To wake in the night, recovering (somewhat) from too much bourbon. To lose one's way to one's own toilet and stumble into a lethal *objet d'art*, crucifying oneself. Even in death Evan had a flair for the theatrical.

Bryce walked outside the 7–11 and kicked the right front tire of his black Chevy Blazer. I'll need to get a new one soon, he thought. And driving down the highway he experienced a quickening of his senses to match the first tingle of fall in the air. Steve had, despite himself, been a useful guest to bring to Jon's party. He had turned from the bar with Katharine's drink just in time to see her slip out the restaurant's front door. Trapped by the crowd it had taken Steve a few minutes to thrash his way to a steamy window where he watched Evan coaxing Katharine down the stairs.

"Walked backward with his hands in his pockets like an infatuated teenager," Steve had reported. "Is that supposed to be charming?"

So Steve had earned a gold star for observation to counter his black mark for charm.

"Is that what working for the FBI does to you?" Bryce had asked. "Makes you an asshole?"

"I'm only an adviser on art," Steve had argued. "And I was only going to compliment her—but did you see how she got her back up right away? Looked at me like I was dirt under her feet."

Bryce had rolled his eyes.

But Steve was on his way to New York, where he belonged. And Bryce was on his way to the Craig residence.

Katharine padded downstairs in a white terrycloth bathrobe; hair, uncombed; face, waking-up pale. She greeted Bryce sleepily and sat at the opposite end of the couch from him, tucking her feet under her. Jon served coffee from a silver service Bryce thought too rich for just a morning chat with the police. But the whole house was a suburban idea of elegance gone wild. Elaborate oversized examples of dark Mediterranean furniture lined the walls. Couches, and there were many, were upholstered in red velvet. Bric-a-brac, often gold-leafed and cherub-trimmed, were as plentiful as weeds on a deserted lot and about as oppressive. Bryce refused the coffee but Katharine had some and let the steam wind around her face as if to catch its fragrance more fully.

Bryce had to repeat his first question twice.

"Sorry," she said, and Bryce thought he saw a tint of red on her cheekbones, though it might only have been the effect of the steam. "Yes, I saw Evan the night I arrived."

"You went with him to his house?"

She seemed surprised. "Yes, I did."

"Did you see anyone else while you were there?"

"No."

"Did he return with you to the party?"

Jon turned his back to them to straighten the photos on the fireplace mantel. He ran one finger along the edge. It came up clean.

"No," she said.

"Did he offer to?"

"Pardon?"

"I mean, it seems unusual for Evan to have let a woman walk alone at night without offering to escort her."

"Meaning Evan never let an opportunity go by to be alone in the dark with a woman," Jon clarified.

She leaned toward the marble-topped coffee table and put sugar in her coffee. "No, he didn't offer."

Bryce gently persisted. "You didn't find that unusual?"

She couldn't completely suppress a smile. "I've always been able to get from point A to point B by myself. I didn't give it a second thought."

Duly chastised, he couldn't help smiling himself. "May I ask why you went to Evan's that evening?"

"May I ask if there's a particular reason for my being questioned on this account?"

"Yes. Evan's been dead since the night of the party. It appears you were the last to see him alive."

She was so still Bryce thought for a moment she might have gone into shock. He made some meaningless doodles in a stenopad. Out of the corner of his eye he saw Jon's head was bent, chin buried in a sweater much too warm for the needs of the morning. One corner of his mouth was visible. It turned up.

"Well, there is a reason then." She took a deep breath. "He wanted me to look at a new sculpture a friend of his had done."

"What sculpture was this?"

"It was called something like *Three Doors*—I don't remember exactly, it was a long title. It was in his bedroom. I suppose you know what I'm talking about if you've been to his house."

"Yes. I know which one," Bryce said tonelessly.

"He asked if I would look at some other things she'd done and I said I would."

"Anything else?"

"No."

"Had he been drinking?"

"Yes. He wasn't too bad though. Just drunk enough to get his courage up."

"Courage up? For what?" Bryce asked quickly.

She shrugged and looked away. Finally, she said, "People, especially people I've brushed off before, don't usually ask me for favors. He really wanted me to look at this woman's work." She was staring at Jon. Jon was giving his attention to a pricey-looking white Persian purring at his feet. "How did Evan die? Was it pills?" The question didn't seem directed toward anyone in particular.

Bryce told her. Her eyes were very large, very gray, and, at that moment, dull. He stood.

"What time did you leave Evan's?"

"Around eleven, I think."

"Did anyone see you return to the party?"

Jon moved back to the fireplace with a cup of coffee.

"I didn't return, really. I met James on the stairs outside the restaurant. James Parnismus, I mean."

And in that second Bryce saw Jon start to turn and catch himself. Bryce quickly pressed the issue.

"You see a lot of James, don't you?"

She gave him one brief nod.

Jon faced him and said, "He's an old family friend, you know."

Bryce smiled. "Everybody does," he said and watched those words trigger a crown of sweat along Jon's hairline. "I can show myself out. Thanks."

Seven

Inga and Petter Swenson had settled in Tahoe fifteen years earlier, emigrating from Sweden. Inga was ten years younger than Petter, a woman of imposing height with thin legs and breasts so large they seemed to upset her balance, the top-heaviness pushing her forward with more speed than she could gracefully control. She often skidded into tables and chairs; even her arms moved quickly, not entirely within her command.

She could usually be found in her kitchen, for she was an enthusiastic cook and collector of kitchen gear. (She'd had her own bakery, a tax write-off for Petter until it actually started showing a profit.) Ceramic molds, copper pans and utensils, gadgets both antique and new, were mounted on the wall, suspended on hooks from under the washed oak cabinets. Otherwise her home reflected a Scandinavian simplicity, a thriftiness. Nestled across the road from the lake in a quiet neighborhood known as Tahoe Park their place was more cottage than house. The floors throughout were the same oak as the cabinets, washed a rosy color. Where rugs were needed they were Chinese; furniture, antique pine, relatively few pieces and *very* good, as was the art displayed on the walls. Modern, in contrast to, yet in keeping with, the spirit of the austere furnishings.

Bryce would stop by a couple of times a week to drink Inga's strong coffee, eat her excellent shortbread as he'd done in her bakery days when they'd first become acquainted, and check on her. Inga was dying and Bryce was one of the few who knew. She'd sold her business, for though she appeared robust at first glance, weaknesses were beginning to show—a tiredness, a tendency to be more emotional than she had previously, a transparency of her skin, and an increasing thinness in her already thin legs and arms. But Inga always smiled, there seemed no changing that. Or the smell of her kitchen, sweet yeast and fresh ground coffee. Bryce hurried in and his ankles were immediately attacked by a Yorkshire terrier, plumped on way too many scraps.

"Brussels the vicious," Bryce said, saving his shin by picking up the animal and scratching his throat. Bug-eyed, the dog gulped gratefully. "No wonder you've never been burglarized, Inga."

Inga threw up her hands, hitting with her finger a copper skillet hanging over the stove.

"No one can arrive unannounced, is this not true?" Inga had the European habit of ending a statement with a question.

"True." He sat down and she put a plate of bread and a cup of coffee before him. They proceeded with their important ritual, food and talk—music or books or world news or, as today, recent events.

"Evan . . ." Inga shook her head. "I thought it was unusual that he missed the party for Katharine. He would never miss a party. Always the first to arrive, yes?"

Bryce looked at her sharply. "You never saw him there?"

"No. Did you?"

No. Come to think of it, he hadn't.

"I looked for him, you see," Inga explained. "He had this artist—what was her name?—Pat, I think. Pat Truscoe. He had been trying to interest Petter and me in a small sculpture of hers. I wanted to tell him we wanted to see it again."

Bryce tapped a spoon against the pine tabletop.

"Can I ask who found the body? Or is that a no-no?" Inga asked.

Bryce smiled. "His friend, Pat Truscoe. She spent last night at the hospital. Finding Evan, in his condition, was a shock for her."

"Gruesome, yes?"

Bryce drank coffee. He didn't need to answer.

"I have something special for—"

Inga was interrupted by the phone. After answering she cupped her hand over the receiver.

"Kevin, this will take a minute. Petter needs information from some papers in the library."

She put the phone on hold and left, Brussels bouncing at her heels. Bryce began tapping with the spoon again. If Evan hadn't attended the party for the sake of partying, then he had come, specifically, for Katharine Craig. "Walking backward with his hands in his pockets" suddenly took on new meaning and raised new questions. Why did he want to talk to Katharine Craig? If it was only to try to push his latest girlfriend into the art world, then why this covert way of approaching her? And if there were another reason, would Katharine be likely to tell it? And could that reason be provocation for her to push Evan in the direction of five hundred eight-inch spikes?

The kitchen door flew open with a bang.

"Inga, I'm absolutely starv—"

Katharine had on a pair of faded jeans and a white cotton shirt, and had her hair caught back, still damp, in a long flat barrette. She was browner than she'd been five days before; he hadn't noticed that in the darker light of Jon's living room. She stopped cold when she saw him sitting at the table.

Not happy to see me? he questioned her silently.

"Excuse me . . . I . . ."

A buzzer went off behind her, loud and tinny. Brussels, barking at a blistering screech, ran back into the room. Bryce took a sip of coffee and said, "Timer's gone off. You might want to take whatever's in the oven out. Inga's upstairs on the phone."

She silenced the timer, proceeded to take the pan from the oven. With her back to him, she asked, "Is this just a friendly visit? Inga hasn't been burglarized, has she?"

"No. Just a friendly visit."

She poured herself some coffee and raised the pot toward him. "Would you like more?"

"Please."

She refilled his cup and sat across from him, quietly fixing her coffee with cream and sugar. Never even jumped when that timer went off, most people would, thought Bryce. Unexpected noise, police in the kitchen, some shocking news not long before. He glanced at his watch. He'd talked to her only forty-five minutes before. She hadn't wasted any time getting out of the house.

"You must have flown," he said.

It took a minute for her to understand his meaning. Then she said, "There's a path between Inga's and our cul-de-sac that comes out behind her house. It's much quicker than taking the road to the highway. If I use my bicycle it's fifteen minutes, maybe."

Inga charged in.

"Ah, Katharine, you're here. Good. You have coffee? Something to eat? There's a plate of things on the table—shortbread, gingerbread—*my timer*." Inga fairly pounced on the oven.

"It's out," Bryce said and Inga's shoulders drooped, presumably in relief. She attacked the contents of another pan with a spatula.

"I want you to take this to that nice Deputy Anderson—it is Anderson, yes?"

Bryce nodded. She slid the contents of the pan into a container already near the full-mark.

"Katharine, *eat*." Inga thrust her spatula into the air. But Katharine only smiled and drank coffee with an expression, Bryce thought, that in anyone with a less straight back, or even with less clear skin, might have been labeled as shy. On her, it simply looked cold. But long years of living with Petter seemed to have conditioned Inga to quiet and cold expressions. She talked continuously—to herself, to Bryce, to Katharine—getting pleasant monosyllables from them and more lavish replies from herself. She also gave a long and detailed account of how Deputy Anderson ("Katharine, you should meet him,'' she said, showing Bryce how it was between the two women) had rescued her Brussels from the cold waters below James' boat at the community Fourth of July picnic. (''Dog's a damned nuisance,'' Bryce whispered, a quiet aside to Katharine who, for an instant, looked less like a baroque saint.)

''There.'' Inga set a grocery bag in front of Bryce as he got up to leave. ''There's more if you don't think this is enough.''

Bryce protested, saying this would be more than enough to fatten every member of the department. But Inga sighed, still not at peace.

''I have made so much, too much. I'm still running the bakery.'' She appealed to Katharine: ''What about James? Can you take some to him? I talked to him this morning and he said you were going to help him—''

''Help him?'' Bryce interrupted with the embarrassed air of one who had missed something in the conversation.

''James asked me to proofread his novel. That's how I'm paying for my sailing lessons.''

''I see,'' Bryce responded tonelessly.

Something in the sergeant's manner had changed in that moment—Katharine's intuition told her so—but with breakfast before her she didn't bother to examine precisely what the change was. Through the front window Inga watched Bryce get into the Blazer and drive away.

''He's a nice man, don't you think? Not bad looking for a man with that kind of reddish hair—one gets used to it. And he's got good coloring—not *too* many freckles.'' Inga told Katharine this as if it were a matter of serious concern. Katharine, whose interest in Bryce's appearance was minimal, bit happily into a thick square of shortbread. ''He's not very tall,'' Inga continued, evidently regarding this as his principal fault. ''But built well,'' she said, alternating to his defense. ''Solid. No *gut*.''

Spoken with her accent the word ''gut'' sounded disreputable and Katharine laughed. Inga turned to her in surprise.

"I'm going to tell Petter you've a wandering eye."

"He knows I'm not looking for me. Too bad about Kevin's wife," she went on, not as an invitation to gossip but as one of her many unfinished thoughts. And contrary to her words, she did not sound particularly sorry. "What do you think? Pleasant, yes? Handsome enough, yes? Lovely voice, isn't it? Very deep and soft."

"I hadn't noticed," Katharine answered truthfully.

Inga sighed and went to the coffeepot. She always found it easier to lecture with a mug of coffee in hand.

"You shouldn't stay so alone, Kat. You should get married. You don't have to have children—or stop traveling—but to have a partnership is a wonderful thing. Especially when you're sick. It's important."

"I'm perfectly healthy—"

"That could all change tomorrow," Inga said, too loudly. Her face trembled at soft stress points: the corners of her mouth, the skin above her eyes. Katharine put down her bread.

"True," she agreed quietly.

Two slender streams of coffee ran down Inga's cup and quickly she set it down. She laughed weakly.

"I apologize . . . Lately, I have been . . . well, never mind. A busybody, I am. Eat," she ordered, which was Inga's solution to everything.

But Katharine was distracted, perhaps on purpose, by a wire set with a handle on each end, hanging on the wall, limp as a marionette.

"That's new, Inga. What's it for? Looks like something out of a mafia movie."

"A cheese wire. You can cut through a fifty-pound wheel of cheese with that." Inga stated this as if it were a matter of pride to cut a fifty-pound wheel properly, should the occasion arise.

"Didn't they use something like that for a murder in *The Godfather*?"

"Katharine, *such* an imagination you have—" She crossed her hands like an umpire calling *safe*, knocking over a tall, wooden pepper mill which landed in a pie tin of flour, flipping that over the edge of the counter onto the head of Brussels, who howled and ran. Inga howled and skidded after him through the kitchen to the living room, through the living room to the dining room and back again. He bounced from chair to chair, over and under, flocking everything with flour as Inga followed behind, loudly apologizing. Brussels also lost control of his bladder before finally wedging himself under an armoire, leaving only his flour-dusted eyebrows, working suspiciously back and forth, in sight.

"Give me that wire and I will strangle him!" Inga, stomach on floor, tried to coax her reluctant Brussels out of hiding. Katharine had been following slowly after, laughing so hard she had tears in her eyes. She let out a yelp when she stumbled back toward the kitchen and ran into an unfamiliar and astonished young man who hadn't been there a moment before. A clipboard fell from his hands and clattered loudly on the floor. Brussels ran out, nipped the man's tennis shoe and ran back under the armoire.

"Bringing the groceries you ordered, ma'am," he gasped.

"Groceries? I didn't order groceries." Inga got up from the floor, still winded.

"I have the order right here," he said. Gathering up his clipboard and pen, he kept one eye on Brussels, who growled. "One gallon cream, two pounds brie, one pound . . ."

Inga snatched the clipboard out of his grubby fingers. He looked up quickly and as he did locks of his blond hair fell into his face. In a vaguely belligerent gesture, he jammed them back. The young man's hair was so pale, so very clean, and the fingers, especially the nails, were so dirty, the contrast caught Katharine's eye. He probably works on cars, she thought irrelevantly. She read the order over Inga's shoulder. It was written in block letters on a sheet of pink receipt-book paper.

Inga pointed to the name at the top of the order. "This

must go to the *Petersons*. We are the Petter Swensons. The Petersons live on the next street."

The young man didn't seem to be paying attention.

"See?" Inga said.

"Yeah. Sorry."

He was athletic looking; brawny but graceful, coordinated. As he left, Katharine watched him through the window. There was a familiarity about this young man. He was a type that used to hang around Jon a lot at one time, though in the days since she'd been back there seemed to be fewer of them. The young man got into a green van and drove away. A moment later he disappeared from Katharine's thoughts.

Eight

Pat Truscoe was not, as Bryce might have supposed, a petite ingenue come into Evan's middle-age to offer rejuvenation, but a woman of forty, hair several shades blonder than was natural to her, thin to the point her skin seemed wound over her bones tight as trampoline leather. Her attractiveness was kept in place by cosmetics applied with an expert hand and by clothes bought at the most expensive shops. But if there was an artificiality to her appearance Bryce did not think there was any to her unhappiness. She sat in his office clutching a disintegrating tissue, answering his questions with dull precision—her address, her occupation (realtor)—and recounted her entry to the house. Browning sat at a computer terminal, as far as Bryce could tell not looking up anything in particular. And Inga's Deputy Anderson, the dutiful disciple of himself and Browning, had come in two hours earlier than he was due for patrol just to hang around investigations. In an office as compact as the Tahoe substation, it was possible for a young deputy with initiative to become involved in any number of departments, from marine duty to SWAT teams. Anderson seemed to have set his sights on investigations. He sat now at one of the desks, pretending to read the list of registered sex offenders.

"You were gone the week?" Bryce asked Pat Truscoe.

"Yes, in San Francisco for a conference. I called him, but . . . when there wasn't any answer I figured he was out. Evan didn't like to be alone." She shrugged. "I saw his car in the garage when I came back. I walked in—"

"Through the garage?"

She nodded.

"Was it locked?"

"No," she said, "Evan never locked any of his doors."

Bryce sat on the corner of his desk and looked at her sharply, though he didn't contradict her.

"I called him . . . began looking through the house . . . it smelled . . ." She swallowed. "I went to the bedroom and saw . . ." Her feet were out of her shoes and she was curling her toes like a nervous child.

"What did you do after that?"

"Screamed."

Bryce smiled, and it was his very nicest smile. "That was sensible," he said.

She took a deep breath. "I ran to the marina restaurant. And Claude, the owner, called you."

Claude had called, all right. His French-accented English was reduced to gibberish when Pat proceeded to throw up all over his kitchen. The ensuing cleaning job held up orders for an hour.

"There's a small point we need to go over. You say Evan never locked his doors."

"He was a careless person."

"His basement was locked."

Pat frowned.

"Did you know that?"

"There was never any reason for me to go to the basement."

"Not even to look at the Picasso there?"

She moved her hands, fluttering scraps of tissue. She shook her head, not only as a gesture of denial, but as one of disbelief. Pat Truscoe was a woman who had matured the hard way and she saw exactly where this line of questioning was headed.

"Like I said, Evan was a careless person. If you think he took those paintings you're out of your mind. You would have caught him by now."

"Then how do you suppose he came by them?"

"I imagine the records would be among his papers, wouldn't you?"

Bryce responded crisply, "Someone got to his papers before I did."

"It wasn't me."

Bryce gave her a tight smile. "You were in San Francisco. Evan had a safe in one of his bedroom closets. Was he also careless about the lock on it?"

"No," she whispered.

"I didn't think so. But it was wide open when we went in. Of course, it makes it difficult to know what's missing since I don't know what was there in the first place."

Pat's eyes were closed.

Bryce said, "You know something that has puzzled me about this area? Real estate. There are almost as many real estate agents as there are trees. Now, that made more sense a few years ago when it didn't take an act of congress to get a building or sewer permit up here. But since that last environmental act—" Bryce shrugged. "Yet, I haven't seen one of you people close up shop. I think that's interesting. Detective Browning, sitting right there behind you, finds that really interesting." Detective Browning beamed. The six-feet-two former Southerner, with just a small thickness to his middle appropriate for his forty-five years, sat back in the chair and gave Pat one courtly nod, a quick wink, when she glanced tentatively in his direction. "Believe me, he has nothing better to do than to sit in front of that terminal and wonder about it." Bryce paused. "And, no, the cocaine hadn't been taken from the safe."

A single mascara-stained tear creased Pat's cheek. Bryce opened a drawer, took out a cigarette and lit it. He passed it to Pat, who sucked on it carefully.

"I'm a businesswoman," she told him. "I understand the principles of business. I understand the principles of exchange. What you don't understand, Sergeant Bryce, is that I don't have anything to offer you."

"Evan was very glib," he said. "He couldn't help talking."

"Maybe. But he didn't fucking *say* anything."

"He didn't have to. He was good at innuendo. That was one of the things that made him so successful with the ladies, wasn't it?"

Through the cigarette smoke Pat narrowed her eyes at Bryce. She gave a dry laugh. "Shit," she said. She dropped the cigarette on the dusty linoleum floor. "This is all I can tell you. I've lived here a little under three years. Evan was one of the first people I met. Like you say, he was a talker. But I've known a lot of talkers in my time and, believe me, I've learned to take it slow. I've worked damned hard to get comfortable and I don't want to risk it on a fast talker. So I took my time with Evan. He was weak, especially with women, but dammit he wasn't mean. A woman like myself can't hope for too much more than that." She leaned forward. "I've been with Evan a year now. In the last six months he was happier but it wasn't just because of me. He and Claude—"

"From the marina?"

She nodded. "They were involved in some business plans together. I don't know exactly what the plans were—I didn't want to know. But I *did* know every time I walked in on them the subject was changed. Until just a few days before I left for San Francisco. I was in the kitchen and they came in from the garage, laughing. Evan asked me how I'd like a trip to France—an extended honeymoon, he called it. I thought he was joking. But then he got a little more specific."

"How specific?"

"He said in three weeks we could fly to Marseilles and then drive through the south of France." She held up her left hand. There was at least two carats' worth of diamonds on her ring finger winking every bit as nicely as Detective Browning.

Bryce let out a long breath. "That was very specific."

"Damn right."

"Do you know any reason why Evan would want or need to see Katharine Craig?"

She sat back in her seat and shrugged. "I don't know Katharine Craig."

"She's Jon Craig's cousin."

That news was nothing to her. "Women were like Everest to Evan. If one was there, he had to try to climb it."

"She said he wanted to show her your sculpture. She's an artist—a good one."

The powdered blush stood out on Pat's cheeks bright as stoplights.

"I have a hobby that pleases no one but me," she said firmly. "Evan—Evan was the type of man who wanted credibility."

Whatever one might call *Three Doors*, Bryce thought—art or garbage, pretentious or profound—there was a grittiness to it that maybe wasn't so far from Pat Truscoe, after all. Bryce looked at her for a moment, then said, "OK. Your car is still at Evan's. If you need a ride anywhere Deputy Anderson will be happy to take you."

She got up. "Please." Stiffly, she hurried out. Deputy Anderson followed after her.

Bryce said to Browning, "Check her San Francisco story, will you?"

Browning gave him a big smile. "My pleasure."

Just as Bryce was getting ready to walk out the door, his phone rang. It was Steve.

"Hey, Daddy, do we have a surprise for you. Your Marin just turned up at the port of Marseilles—"

Bryce sat back down. "Well, isn't that convenient?"

Nine

Bryce took Deputy Martin Anderson with him to question Claude Roux. With a name like Martin Anderson, Bryce thought, he ought to be a long-limbed blond, someone clean and solid and rosy-cheeked. Anderson was long-limbed, all right. But that was where the Nordic similarity ended. He had straight black hair cropped boot-camp short, skin just the creamier side of jaundice, and a face pitted by a case of acne that in its heyday must have been painful enough to bring him to tears. His eyes were clear blue with an almond slant, testifying to a mixed ethnic background. His arms were as slender and undefined as a girl's—a six-foot-five girl. And it was Bryce's opinion that he must have suffered some of the same adolescent cruelty as a girl of that unusual height. Bryce didn't know if Anderson's singling out had been due to his mixed race, his acne, or even to something earlier in life, more complex. Bryce only knew that Anderson was a young man who took all criticism seriously, viewed praise with suspicion and did what he was told without complaint. Conscientious, yes. But too quick to get physical. And, despite his slenderness, he was strong; during tense confrontations Bryce kept one eye on him. Bryce also liked to see how people would respond to Anderson's presence. He used him like the point of a compass, to tell which direction a person's mind might run.

Claude, dark haired, fine boned and five feet two if he stretched on his toes, received them in an office hardly bigger than a closet, so that he had to position himself in a corner to view Anderson in his entirety.

"I take it this is not a social visit, Kevin? You do not come to compliment me on the vichyssoise?"

"It's great, Claude, for cold potatoes."

Claude snorted, put his lips to the top of a bottle of Vittel and took them away without drinking. "Bullshit," he said, not referring to his soup. "When the authorities come in pairs it is for a purpose."

"Which is?"

Claude jerked his handsome head toward Anderson. "One to intimidate, one to question. In your case, it is my opinion one would be enough."

"Everyone likes a little support."

"Can I call in my kitchen help then? Yes? No?"

"No."

Claude shrugged. "We will be straightforward, yes?"

Bryce doubted it, but he nodded anyway.

"Evan is dead, yes? It was an accident?"

"We need the results of the autopsy report to determine that for sure."

"And if the gossip is correct, Evan was found with stolen merchandise—paintings—on his property." Claude held up one hand as if to stop Bryce from taking offense, to assure him he understood the position of the authorities was to question, not to be questioned. "I want to be sure I understand the facts."

"Understanding them and knowing them are two different things," Bryce said.

"You are very precise with your language, Kevin."

"It's important to be precise with what you know. Or understand."

The atmosphere was thick with air in which garlic-tainted oil, steam from poached seafood, and the sizzling fat of steaks had evaporated. It was made closer still by the odor of sweat—Claude's.

"You were planning to go to Marseilles with Evan. What was the purpose of the trip?"

"A visit to the homeland with friends is perhaps not so surprising, is it?"

"That depends on what he knows—or understands—about the trip, doesn't it? Or the friends he's planning to travel with."

"And what do you know or *understand* about the man who is dead, Kevin?"

"Not enough," Bryce answered quietly.

"Then I will tell you." Claude settled behind his desk. He knew how to use his hands beautifully, punctuating his thoughts with long smooth sweeps of his fingers. He started with an index finger, straight up, just discreet enough not to be an accusation. "You are not a social man, Kevin. I see you at the bar sometimes. You talk, say what is necessary. You are friendly, but do not appear to be seeking friends. I do not know how much understanding you will have for someone like Evan. He would talk, *mon Dieu*, he would talk and say nothing. Women didn't seem to mind. He was gentle with women—he *liked* them. What you must understand is that all his compliments were sincere so they responded in kind. But men, he made suspicious. Maybe he tried too hard, dressed too much like a magazine advertisement. And what was his business? He owned hairdressing salons—two on the south shore, one in Tahoe City. If he hadn't been sleeping with many of their wives at one time or another they would have thought him—" Claude raised his eyebrows, rocked his hand from side to side. "You see, their suspicion was not the result of his women, but of the fact that Evan was not what most men felt a woman—*their* woman—ought to desire. If they are to be cheated on let it be with the big strong example of a man, not the Pillsbury Doughboy, not the flamboyant hairdresser, yes?"

"The point you're making is that Evan was not accepted."

"That is the word," Claude responded excitedly. "Tolerated, yes. Accepted, no. For some of us to be different is easier than others. We find our compensations." Claude's eyes rested on Anderson, perhaps with a less utilitarian perspective. "Generally, I think, Evan enjoyed women so much the men were not a concern. However . . . he could still be hurt. If the snub was pointed enough. If it came from the right source."

Bryce asked, "Was he snubbed by the right source?"

"I believe so. But he was not precise. I cannot offer you details."

"Are you trying to give me a motive for suicide?" Bryce was sharply disbelieving.

Claude ventured, ever so quietly, his carefully balanced, imprecise answer.

"No, for meanness."

"Meanness? What sort of meanness?"

Claude was drinking mineral water as if he were very thirsty.

"Live and let live is a good philosophy. Evan tried to live by it," he said, dabbing the corners of his mouth with his fingertips.

"And you're saying one day he didn't live by it and this might be the result? You want me to understand that, but you don't want to give me anything concrete—no name, no places, no dates."

"That is because I don't know anything concrete. I was a friend, but not a good enough friend to become involved." He licked his lips. His tongue was very small and red and darted quickly in and out as if it shouldn't be exposed at all.

Bryce put his hands on the desktop and leaned forward. "Bullshit," he said.

"I'm trying to help."

"Sure. And cover your ass at the same time. It doesn't work, Claude. A couple of days ago, four stolen works of art from Tahoe were picked up in Marseilles. Do you have a friend, or a cousin, or a brother, or an old business associate who doesn't mind something to the left of the law if it pays well enough?"

Claude's eyes held Bryce's, steady, dark brown, without regrets. "I own a restaurant, that is my business, my first love."

"I have a question for you, Claude. Why was it Pat who found Evan and not you? When he didn't show up at the bar for three days, didn't you wonder where he was?"

"I thought I knew where he was. He talked of surprising Pat in San Francisco. Something to do with her art. He had, I think, something of a romantic gesture in mind."

Bryce was not certain if Claude's dry delivery was meant to show disdain for Pat's art or for romantic gestures. Perhaps he had a practical disapproval for both.

"This snub, you're saying it came from a man, then?"

Claude appeared puzzled. "I know it came from someone he admired and I have always believed a woman was involved. But I cannot believe that a woman would be the object of such anger. He was unusually—what is the word?—indirect."

What was it Katharine Craig had said that morning? thought Bryce. *People I've brushed off before.*

"Money is a funny thing," Claude said. "It does not buy happiness but it can bring a certain comfort. Evan had money enough to make life pleasant."

"Maybe he was looking for a different kind of comfort."

"There isn't any."

A sound came from behind Bryce. He half turned, surprised because though Anderson was good at provoking responses, except for an occasional punch or knee to the crotch, he rarely had any himself. But Anderson stood with his eyes on his notebook, his posture neutral. Bryce would have wondered if he'd only imagined the noise if Claude hadn't seemed to give Anderson a brief, sympathetic glance.

Bryce said to Claude, "You seem to have spent too much time with Evan. You've picked up some of his bad habits. When you decide to say what you mean, give me a call, will you?"

Ten

"Dammit, James, proofreading!"

Bryce's voice was too low-pitched, too melodious to actually yell. But it did contain an unusual intensity. James Parnismus peered out of a porthole, apparently undisturbed.

"Let me tell you a story, Kevin. It's a story about a writer." James was always his most coherent when speaking in the story form. Bryce looked up at the ceiling. "Now, in the folly of his youth, struggling with his first eager, overwritten sentences and bad ideas, circumstances brought this writer a partner. A damn good partner. He could write a terrific sentence, bounce ideas around all day long, could keep some of this writer's more farfetched ideas in check and could even spell, by God. Together they wrote one novel and then another and then another, and then, lo and behold, began a fourth. And you know what was really nice? The books sold. They made *money*. Like in a fairy tale. But—" James mocked an ominous expression "—to every fairy tale there is a darker side. And the worm in this apple is that this partner has a job, a serious job, a distracting job. And because it's distracting, this partner is not keeping up his end of the bargain—"

"Bullshit," Bryce interrupted.

"Only partially. The story isn't over yet. But first let me articulate: the books, which may have started out as just a way of entertaining ourselves during the long cold winters, are now a job. So you have two. I mean, can you remember the last time you met a woman and asked her to dinner? Probably not. So you pushing yourself isn't anything new. What is new is that you're working on an exceptionally odd case and have somehow managed to involve me by persuading me to keep a woman I've known since she was twelve—''

About this time Bryce expected James to lose his train of thought. He usually did.

''—You want Kat to stick around, fine—'' James, the connection between his brain and his mouth failing him, stopped talking.

After a short, frustrated silence Bryce supplied the appropriate words. ''You feel like a prick.''

''That, and slightly idiotic,'' he said, putting his hands in his pockets and his backside against the navigational desk. Bryce was sitting on the blue cushions surrounding the galley table, one heel on the padding. ''She looks at me like she's humoring me. She *is* humoring me. And I don't understand the purpose—''

''Right. So I'm going to tell you. Jon Craig confessed to the burglaries the night of Katharine's coming-home party.''

On James' face Bryce saw an odd mix of surprise and belief. ''Is he in custody?''

''He confessed to me privately without any intention of giving himself up.''

James' response this time was dry and completely without surprise. ''And you've got no physical evidence and Evan's dead with a basement full of stolen art.''

''Right, again.''

James whistled through his teeth and looked at Bryce with a gaze that was not without suspicion. ''Why are you telling me?''

Because I'm going to use you, Bryce wanted to say. But it was one of those things that was probably self-evident. Bryce had always kept James and their joint books private and separate from his police work. Now he was going to put that comfortable place at risk.

''Because you're probably one of the few people in this community who'll believe me. I don't know why you don't like Jon, but I know you have reservations about him.''

James stalled. Despite a generally well-scrubbed public

appearance, James was a slob at home. The galley counters and table were forested with empty beer bottles and mustard-crusted knives. Scraps of paper, stained and scribbled on, were snowed with flakes of croissant. Bryce picked up a pair of barbecue tongs, red sauce dried on its claws.

James said, "You can walk away from a fight, especially a stupid one."

Tongs poised mid-air, Bryce stared at him. But James went on quite reasonably.

"You don't need this. The books make money enough—God knows, your needs are simple. Pray tell, when was the last time you bought a shirt? 1983?"

"It's not that simple."

"Yes, it is. We could sail the boat to Tahiti, find two gorgeous native girls and live happily ever after." They remained quiet. Finally, James sighed. "Do you think Evan was a fence?"

Bryce shook his head. "I don't know. I find it difficult to accept. He had a wall safe in a closet. The door was wide open. But I don't know what was in there. There's an unidentified pair of fingerprints on the closet door, but they won't turn out to be Jon's. Which reminds me, what time did you meet Katharine on the stairs?"

"Around eleven. It wasn't too long after you left."

"How did she look? Upset in any way?"

"No, just exhausted. Did Jon have time to go to Evan's between the time Katharine left the house and he arrived at the Mathesons'?"

"It's possible. And for all we know he didn't necessarily arrive after she left."

"If Katharine had just witnessed Evan pincushioned against that door, Kevin, I don't think she would have fallen asleep on my shoulder. Not even Kat is that cool."

"She could have left before that happened."

James went to the refrigerator. He wrenched the cap from a frosty bottle of Labatt's and planted his elbows on the counter, setting one in a Hershey's kiss of jam. "Katharine is one of the most truthful women I have ever known. If she says something, you can bet, to the best of her knowledge, it's the truth. It's more what she doesn't say you have to watch."

"I didn't ask if Jon was there."

"Then you didn't ask the right question, did you?" James stood straight and took a long drink.

"Evan only had twentieth-century pieces, not one nineteenth-century piece in the lot. A few works, including my Marin, were picked up at the port of Marseilles the other day. They were also only twentieth-century pieces. What does that say to you?"

James drank, pacing the whole of the three economical feet the teak-lined galley allowed him.

"An unorthodox method of paying blackmail."

"Jon's an eloquent bastard, isn't he? Even when he's not talking. Leaves that safe door wide open to say: 'Fuck you, idiot. Old Evan could get evidence you couldn't. And I even beat you at getting that back.' "

James stopped, looking at him. "Evan had a bit of, in the light of recent events, rather dubious luck that you didn't have."

But Bryce did not appear eager to encourage comfort. He said, "Everything found in Evan's basement was identified by the Mathesons except for two small sculptures. Now, in Evan's living room there's a chrome case and from it something had been removed. If you measure the base of this something by the dust ring it more or less corresponds to the base size of these two sculptures."

"So you think there was a third sculpture?"

"It looks like it."

"In his *living* room? No wonder he got on Jon's nerves."

Bryce laughed a little. "They're whimsical little pieces, these sculptures—only six inches tall. Bronze macaws that are more human than birdlike. It's as if the artist had—"

James was choking, frantically waving his hands, spreading beer over the counter like fat drops of sour rain. "Those are Kat's," he coughed out. "And I mean *hers*. Never shown to the public. In fact, I don't think anyone but Jon and I have ever seen them."

"You're sure?"

"As sure as I can be without seeing them," he said, still heaving.

"Then you better see them," Bryce said quietly.

"You want me to come down to the station?"

Bryce ignored the question. "I didn't get much of a chance to talk to Katharine. Between Steve spouting off and Jon stepping in, she couldn't get away fast enough. Perhaps because I'm a relative newcomer there may be things you know, that you take for granted, that I may not know—things that may be helpful. For example, from just the little I've seen I think there's some kind of unusual relationship between Jon and Katharine. Were they lovers?"

"What on earth makes you think—?"

"Because of the way he touches her," Bryce said, using his most academic voice. And James, as Bryce knew he would, tried to match this calmness.

"I find that difficult to believe."

"This morning, when I questioned her, Jon was there. When she said she'd been with Evan, he didn't bat an eye. But when he found out you took her home I thought he was going to go through the roof. Do you know why?"

James let out a deep breath. "Yes and no. I don't know why he cares, but I know he doesn't like my relationship with Katharine, never has. It took me years to figure that out, believe me. When I was a teenager I took his friendliness pretty much the way everyone else does, as genuine."

"What changed that?"

James didn't have a shirt on, only a pair of white shorts, and socks on each foot, one white and one pastel argyle. He walked back to the navigational desk, scratching his back.

"I didn't leave for college right after I graduated from high school, I waited a year. After I turned eighteen Jon started making jokes, jokes just pointed enough to embarrass

Kat, about how she was underage and I better be careful. She and I spent a lot of time together—her mom had died in a car accident that year and her dad, well, he was coming down with the illness that eventually killed him. She used to follow me around—she was only a kid—had a crush on me, I suppose, though even then it wasn't easy to tell. I didn't mind having her around, she wasn't much of a nuisance. Anyway, Jon's teasing was consistent enough to irritate me. So I said something to him finally and he gave me a prolonged lecture on good sportsmanship—"

Bryce waited, his chin propped on the heel of his hand, fingers discreetly over his mouth.

"—and I was almost convinced I was an ass when I found Jon's hand rubbing the inside of my thigh."

Bryce was laughing. "I would give anything to have seen your face."

"It wasn't a pretty sight, I can tell you."

Bryce couldn't resist. "It must have been pretty enough for Jon."

An empty beer bottle whizzed by his head and landed damage-free in a sweat-shirt stashed on the shelf behind the seat.

"You know, it's one thing if someone you know to be gay does something like that. But when it comes from someone like Jon who—how do I say this?—makes no claims in that direction and doesn't even seem especially tolerant of gay people, then it gets ugly. To this day I'm not sure if he was really interested or if he just wanted to see if he could manipulate me. Maybe he thought I'd be so upset I wouldn't come around, even to see Kat. I don't know. I *do* think that it wasn't just me. I think he is—or was—possessive of her."

"You must irritate the hell out of him," Bryce said softly. "No matter what his motives, that kind of action leaves him vulnerable. And, on top of it, your relationship with Katharine continues. No wonder he jumps."

James was about to ask a question. It was a question Bryce dreaded, yet knew had to come eventually. But Bryce also knew if he could boggle James' thought processes long enough, he could get out of answering it today.

Bryce said, "James, domestic situations are very tricky things. I know you probably don't think Katharine is involved with Jon's burglaries. If you're right, do you think, if I was straightforward with her, that she would cooperate with me?"

Poor James. Bryce could tell he didn't like answering, didn't like having his loyalties divided. Whatever his attachment to Katharine—and it was an attachment Bryce didn't completely understand—Bryce knew it was one to which James applied all his inborn chivalry. He watched James the realist war with a lot of wishful thinking.

"I think she'd get the hell out of here," James said finally.

Angry, not at one another, but each for their own reasons at the situation, they were silent for a moment, pensive. And it was this unhappy feeling they held in common that was apparent as a quick knock on the cabin door heralded the descent of long legs down the stairs. Katharine didn't seem surprised to see Bryce this time. She stopped, a small leather gym bag slung over her shoulder. She had traded the jeans for a pair of crisp white shorts.

"Checking up on my story, Sergeant?" she said, friendly enough.

He smiled. "It's my job," he said.

She glanced from one man to the other. With one arm she shoved some of the mess on the counter over and set the bag in a puddle of beer and mustard.

They make a helluva pair, Bryce thought. One slob for another.

Katharine got a beer, then patted James' rump to get him to move and stood next to him. Side by side, two against one.

Bryce brought a photograph out of his shirt pocket. To Katharine he said, "Do you recognize this man? It's an old snapshot, I know."

She took the photo then went back to her place beside James. Bryce wondered if she could feel the sudden tenseness in James. She must, Bryce could *see* it. James' flat stomach turned tight as a washboard. For, of course, over her shoulder, James recognized the photo. It was a picture of Bryce's stepfather at age thirty-seven.

"I'm sorry, I don't," she said. She made to return it but Bryce was occupied with the tongs once more, so she placed the photo on the edge of the table. James took her beer and drank from it.

"Do me a favor, will you, Kat? There's a T-shirt laying on the captain's bed. Would you get it for me, please?"

She looked sideways at him, and silently, without hurry, went to fetch it. Using the tongs, Bryce returned the photo to his pocket.

When Katharine returned with the shirt (probably had her choice of a dozen strewn all over the bed, Bryce thought) he made to leave. But before he did, standing in those close quarters quite near to them, he asked, "Miss Craig, was Jon at Evan's house at any time while you were there that evening?"

She looked him straight in the eye. "No."

As Bryce walked down the docks he made a mental note of two points. One was the way Katharine Craig had walked onto James' boat, hardly knocking, completely at ease. He wondered if those bird sculptures were really hers and, if they were, why she hadn't reported them missing. And then there was the way she touched James. She used a playful, sexless tag, the kind one might use patting the hind end of a favorite child. He couldn't help wondering what her reaction would be if she found one of those missing sculptures in James' possession—if it might be a reaction he could use in some way.

Bryce had made a note of one other small point.

She sure smelled good.

Eleven

The road was lousy. Potholed and creviced, lacking either asphalt or gravel, it was just the way Bryce liked it. At the top of the hill was home, a half-mile from the nearest neighbor, backed by National Forest. His grandparents had purchased the property many years before, when property was still cheap. A cabin was built, used for holidays, and neglected after their death until an incredible combination of bureaucratic manipulation and luck had transferred him here five years before. His grandparents had been quiet people, not social, and his own visits to them rare—as a youngster because of some rift between grandparent and parent that neither side felt it their business to relate to him; and later because he was busy with his own life, supporting a son, and eventually a wife, too. As a result his relationship with his grandparents had the sweetness of a honeymoon, each memory perfect. Perhaps he had been hoping this feeling might rub off on his marriage. Yet somehow he wasn't disappointed that it hadn't, as if living in this cabin, alone, had been his unconscious goal all along.

Bryce stood on the front porch and rolled down the sleeves of his flannel shirt. He was glad summer was a short season in the Sierras, and happier still it was coming to a close. He liked the fall, he liked the winter and the chores that went with them: the wood chopping, the snow shoveling, the skiing when the road home was impassable by car. It provided the best atmosphere for his favorite indoor occupations: listening to music, reading, working on his own books, drinking hot brandy. His cabin was old Tahoe, built of logs; one large window in the front room gave him a panoramic view of the lake, a small one in the kitchen gave him a scaled-down version of the same. A black bear rug, bear shot and tanned by his grandfather, stretched out before a stone fireplace within a toe-reach of a thick-tufted gray sofa. Next to a leather wingback chair was a badly scarred table of burled walnut. A stand-up lamp was positioned over the shoulder, specifically for reading. The wall surrounding the fireplace was covered with a bookcase. Up a set of stairs, narrow and steep as if designed for a mountain goat, was a bedroom and an incredibly uncomfortable bathroom, caught on the steep side of the roof so that he had either to sit or hunch over in the shower. The bedroom was as Spartan as he could manage: an iron bed, a nightstand, a cedar chest full of blankets, a large flat-topped pine desk. The house was much the same in his grandparents' day. His wife had left no impression on it, as though she'd known all along she was only a temporary resident.

But even here, in the place where he was usually the most content, he felt dissatisfied. For he knew that he and Claude shared the same fear. That the thief, the probable murderer, had played his naughty trick and would now do the sensible thing and stop. Not because he was sensible, but because he was a perfectionist. Each of his crimes was as well-formed as a pearl and the string of them were now clasped neatly together by Evan's death. Evan would, at least in the public's mind, be credited with the burglaries, his death attributed to a horrible accident. And, unless he could come up with some physical evidence to the contrary, that would also be the official verdict. Claude must have suspected this and his sense of outrage was what spurred his own vague information this afternoon. But whatever else Claude did know, Bryce felt sure he did not know the identity of the thief. Claude was a practical man, not fool enough to think himself safe if he knew that information.

Bryce went to the kitchen, got ice from the fridge, sweet well water from the tap, then went back outside and sat on the top step of the porch. It was funny, being alone. Most of the time it was comfortable enough. But then one day, and maybe just for one day, it wasn't all right. There were things he didn't like about being married, things he didn't like about being alone. There were days he felt, in divorcing his wife, he had merely traded one inconvenience for another. James was going out this evening or he might have called him, asked him to bring the manuscript. Though Bryce didn't try to fool himself. The kind of comfort desired was not to be found between the pages of a book, or even in the companionship of a friend like James.

The glass was sweating in his hand, he sipped it gratefully. Inga was having a party that night for her wedding anniversary. He could go, if he was that interested in company. But Jon would be there and Bryce would have to be polite and, remembering the way Evan's body had hung on that door, Bryce didn't think he had that much politeness in him. His disposition was too precarious to be tested by Jon's vanity. He thought if there was an imperfection to Jon's moves it lay in the fact that Evan would get credit for Jon's cleverness, and Bryce wondered how Jon would cope with that, if it might be his undoing.

He certainly hoped so.

Twelve

"Imagine twenty years together," Jon said, then tasted his champagne. "It's a rarity we're witnessing, Katharine. Not just twenty years, but twenty years of being honest and faithful, in their case."

"Very unusual." She stood a little apart from him, accepted his comments knowing his emphasis was on the faithful, hers on the honest and neither of them on the situation in hand.

Inga and Petter were celebrating their anniversary at home with a few friends. Petter, handsome in white cotton slacks, pastel plaid shirt and a white sweater, looking as if he were ready to go yachting, was easing himself from Inga's side, one eye toward the kitchen. Inga was pretty in a flowered full skirt and a high-collared Victorian blouse. Sipping champagne with James, Inga's head was tipped near to his and they were laughing.

"Halloween's only a couple of weeks away. Are you going to be here for my party?" Jon asked.

"It looks like it," she said.

"Give me a hand, maybe?"

It was an involuntary gesture, taking that extra half-step away from him. "If you like." She smiled, but knew better than to act apologetic. If she was, he would consider her weak. If she spoke her mind, she would be labeled demanding. It was her choice to stay evasive and defy any of his descriptions.

Jon considered his glass.

"Coming as Guinevere again this year?"

"Do you have to ask?"

"I shouldn't. You've been using the same costume for eight years. Ever since you were Guinevere in that amateur thing in—where was it? England?"

"It was a satire, you would have liked it."

"I would not," he said, amused, assured. "King Arthur was so tacky and so stupid running after Grails. I prefer Julius Caesar. The Romans, at least, had baths. The English never bathed."

"That's my Jon, always looking out for his creature comforts."

"And why not? I can make a very good case for my creature comforts. Better than you could for your bohemianism."

"You could make a convincing case for Attila the Hun, if you wanted. I've always thought it a shame you didn't go into law. And I think 'bohemian' is an archaic classification for my lifestyle," she said. How typical of him to choose this moment to place his digs; close enough to the public to guarantee civility, far enough away not to be overheard.

"Do you really? Have you ever looked up 'bohemian' in the dictionary—"

"Have you? That seems a strange thing to be doing with your very expensive time."

"It's a gypsy."

She smiled, already tired. "Surely there's nothing disreputable about not staying in an American hotel or taking a freighter instead of a Princess cruise."

Summoning all of his extensive dignity, he said, "I prefer not to speculate on what may go on during these excursions."

"Jon-a-than," she said, trying to keep the banter lighthearted. She felt a change in attitude, sharp and dangerous as a needle prick at her heart.

"Tell me why you find it so difficult to join in? To settle down? Just a logical reason, that's all I'm asking." Jon always sounded his most reasonable when he was actually his least. But what surprised her was that she wasn't angry with him. She wondered on which visit that had changed, if the indifference had come so slowly it had been there a long time without her realizing. She felt sad that the one point of strong emotion in her life was reduced to a commonplace annoyance. There was an eyelash laying on his cheek and without thinking she moved to brush it away. But as quickly as she backed away from his talk, he backed away from her touch.

Petter wheeled out a tea-cart. On it was a three-tiered cake and a package wrapped with cloth and blue ribbon. He held out his hand to Inga.

"I have a surprise for you," he stated gravely.

Inga's hand shook and, knowing how clumsy she could be, guests held their breath. Even Petter looked strained. But the wrapping slipped to the floor without casualty.

The gift had been painted in the late nineteenth century. The background was lush, filled in with rich textured draperies and Oriental rugs. An arrangement of flowers had been detailed to the finest shadow. A beautiful woman sat taking her tea surrounded by fruit more luscious than was ever found at the local supermarket; little cakes sat temptingly on china plates. The woman, dressed in green velvet and lace, gazed at the party, aristocratic, beyond touch in her gilded frame.

Inga blinked and stared. And when she whispered to Petter his face relaxed. The rest of the party joined in expressing their approval, tactfully not stating the obvious sentiment—how lucky the thief is no longer among us. Everyone smiled and drank champagne.

Except for James. It was so unusual for James to leave a drink unfinished that Katharine couldn't help noticing. And to eat cake, he didn't like cake. She watched him eat a sugar rose and gag. He put down his plate and said, "I'm going home. Can I give you a lift?"

"Just let me say good-night to Inga," she said.

She found Inga in the kitchen.

"Ah, Katharine, have you met Martin? Martin Anderson

this is Katharine Craig,'' Inga said, introducing the man at her side.

Katharine's eyes went, not to the scars on his face, but to his eyes. Clear blue, not unlike those of Jon's fat Persian cat, there was something about them that gave her pause. She shied away from shaking his hand and said her goodbye to Inga, who was twisting the cheese wire in her hand. Jon and Petter were cloistered near the coffeepot, deep in conversation. Katharine decided not to disturb them. Jon would find out soon enough she'd left without him. He ought to expect it.

James knew he'd be invited in. They went directly to her studio, as they always did. It was as if Katharine was uncomfortable with any other section of the house except for this sparsely furnished workroom. Perhaps there was too much of Jon in the other ones: too much oversized furniture, too many gee-gaws. This room had nothing but a worktable, tools and smocks hanging on the wall, a drafting desk, closets, a sink, an electric burner and plenty of light and space. He remembered at the time how indulgent it seemed for Jon to build such a room for a schoolgirl, even one who had lost her mother, father, and guardian—Jon's father—all within eighteen months. And James still couldn't completely deny the generosity, though he wondered if it was just that Jon was incapable of doing anything that wasn't on a grand scale. This night he found a disturbing element in the room. It was clean. Not one half-finished sculpture, not a dirty smock or a clay-encrusted tool, no series of half-empty teacups, or crushed potato chips on the floor. He had a wild urge to turn the table over, scatter the tools from their hooks, maybe shred a smock with his bare hands. Instead, he said, ''I've been interrupting your work, Kat.''

She was heating water on the electric burner, preparing two cracked mugs with pre-mixed chocolate. ''Thank God,'' she said. James felt his mouth drop open slightly. ''Does that surprise you, James?'' she asked kindly.

''Yes . . . and no. I mean, it seems you ought to be tired,

you've been working like a maniac ever since—" James searched for the most diplomatic assessment and finally settled on the simple calculation of years "—well, since you were seventeen or eighteen. So after ten years of being a workaholic I'd expect you to be tired. But since you've never shown any sign of being tired, it comes as a surprise. Does that make sense?"

"Somewhat," she said. "I've enjoyed myself, James."

He nodded rather nervously, leaning against the wall. "You were meant to. Do you remember—" he had his eye on a particular closet door "—that bird Inga used to have. The macaw?"

She smiled sweetly. "The one who bit Jon?"

James laughed. "I'd forgotten that. Made his finger bleed, didn't it?"

"Took a hunk out of his thumb. It could be friendly when it was in the mood. It's funny it didn't like Jon, most animals do—they respond to authority, I suppose. But it was an independent little bugger. Very intelligent, too. Made a big impression on me."

"Things did, then." He hadn't meant to say that. It was one of the rare occasions when his thoughts bubbled to his mouth ungarbled. But as if to underline his point she didn't laugh, didn't seem upset, didn't question his meaning.

"It's an impressionable age," she said.

Katharine, you don't have to be cagey with me! But this explosion did get lost along the way. He said, "I don't remember what happened to it. I came back from college one spring break and it was gone."

"Inga found it with its neck broken."

James felt his stomach lurch. It was too much to expect her to be emotional after all these years but her deadpan delivery made him unaccountably furious.

"I've been thinking about getting a bird for the boat. Good company. Also, it completes the yo-ho-ho and a bottle of rum picture."

She laughed. "It's a very romantic notion, James. Until the first morning you wake up and put your toe in birdshit."

"Getting shit on generally is the price you pay for romance," he said.

"Yo-ho-ho," she said. "I did a series of the bird from some sketches I'd done years ago, before he died. I think I showed them to you, didn't I?"

"Yes, they were lovely." Perhaps the excitement of finally leading the conversation where he wanted it to go, and his suppressed irritation with her, served to infuse this ordinary sentence with some special intensity.

Katharine glanced at him. "Let me make you a present of one, James."

He reacted appropriately. He couldn't speak. Partly because he was so surprised; those sculptures were among her favorites. Partly because he felt guilty.

She tugged on his sleeve. "Come on, don't be noble. Take advantage of me in a weak moment."

He watched her at the closet. His was an odd reaction to such naked dismay. A flood of relief and then, *Good*, he thought. *Good, good. Scream. Yell. Ask why.*

But she remained as empty of sound as her closet was of sculpture.

Thirteen

Katharine sat silently contemplating a glass of wine as Bryce and his associates made their investigation of the house. She could hear the murmur of their voices, sometimes loud, sometimes low, sometimes overhead, sometimes out in the yard. They seemed everywhere at once. She heard the opening and closing of cabinets, the shuffle of furniture being moved. And through her wineglass she watched the gradual undoing of James' boat shoe laces as he paced before the fireplace. Suddenly, he was leaning over her.

"You've destroyed that wine, holding the glass instead of the stem. In my opinion if you're going to spend more time *looking* at a wine than drinking it, you're better off with a red—something that holds up to room temperature. Cabernet? Too heavy for four in the morning. Port? Too obnoxious for any time. How about a nice Pinot Noir?"

He took her glass, went to the bar and poured her a fresh one. Coming back, he knelt before her and positioned her hand around the glass.

"Now let's swish this around so all those alcoholic thing-amabobbers can beat against one another. Good. Now, take a whiff." Like a well-behaved child, she obeyed. "Good girl! Take a sip and let it ooze over your whatchamacallit."

Once again, she did as instructed.

"Taste good? Did you notice the black cherry quality? The label said it had one."

She finally had to laugh.

A caravan of police came down the stairs. James stood

as Bryce joined them. The rest of the crew found their way out.

"We already have a statement from you," he said to James. "I'd like to talk to you again, Miss Craig. Can we talk privately?"

"Of course," she said.

Obviously reluctant to leave them alone, James said, "Do you want me to stay on?"

She squeezed his hand. "No. You better get some sleep."

James looked at Bryce, who was carefully avoiding him. After a second of indecision James kissed Katharine on the cheek and left.

Bryce pulled a chair close, a stenopad and pencil in hand, and approached her seriously.

"Is there any other place your sculptures could be?"

"No. It's rare for me to keep my work. If it doesn't go into a gallery or it's not commissioned, I have a storage studio in an artist's coop." She paused. "I did call Jon to see if he had moved them for some reason."

"He hadn't?"

"He'd forgotten they were here."

Something in her manner suggested what to him? Puzzlement? Disbelief? Reluctance of some sort?

"Is there anything else?" he asked carefully.

"Oh, no. Once I finish a project I lose interest in it usually, so there's no reason for him to remember either." She shrugged. "I don't often discuss my work with him."

"Where is Jon?"

"Still at the Swensons', I suppose."

"He's not coming home?"

"Eventually. He usually does."

"Does he sometimes not come home?"

"Sometimes."

"When he doesn't come home, where does he go?"

"I don't ask."

And don't care, thought Bryce.

"When was the last time you saw the sculptures?"

For a moment Bryce wondered if she was going to cry. She didn't.

"Let's see. I haven't even thought to look at them since I've been back—and I hadn't been here since when?" She closed her eyes, rubbed the sudden creases on her forehead. "Wait. Last Halloween. That's when I was here last, that's when I saw them."

"You're sure?" he said, though her attitude left no doubt.

"Yes."

"Do you remember the circumstances?"

She didn't answer right away and when she did her words were painfully succinct.

"I felt like looking at them and got them out."

Bryce wondered if he should let that go. He scribbled meaningless doodles in his notebook and tried a different approach.

"You have a very casual attitude toward your things."

"Pardon?"

He was friendly. "I mean, I don't think either you or Jon ever lock your doors, for instance. Much less turn the alarm system on—for all the good they've been doing lately. Although I can't imagine any local hoodlums bothering him. With his intelligence system he would track them down in no time."

She smiled at this completely correct and unromantic assessment of Jon's influence. "I don't know what they would take. There really isn't any valuable art here—unless they decided to haul away the furniture, which they could do with my blessing," she finished wistfully.

"You don't like the furniture?" It was best, especially now when she was tired, to keep her talking. And she had a way of speaking, not quite British, no longer entirely American, that intrigued him.

"I despise it. Sorry, I'm sure you don't want my opinion on the furniture."

"If that's the case, I'm surprised the two of you don't argue over it."

"I've always considered this house Jon's so there's never

an argument. I'm not here enough to get pushy and most of the time I blank out what's here anyway. I've had years of practice at it."

"Is the house his? Legally, I mean?"

She paused, considering him. "Half of it—the other half's mine."

"Never bought a place of your own?"

"What for?"

"It's a good investment."

She smiled wryly. "You sound like James."

"Some people just like a place to call home," he persisted gently. "A place to store what they have."

"I don't have much. Hardly more than my clothes and my tools, in fact."

"And your birds."

"And now they're gone, too."

He understood the ironic tone, if not completely the irony behind it.

"How about the housekeeper—would she have access to your studio?"

"Jon has some kind of housekeeping service but the studio is kept locked. Only Jon and I have a key though he doesn't go in there—all the dust and garbage that collect in it irritate him. He was going to turn on the alarm when I started working."

"You haven't started?"

"No. I've been busy . . . and unmotivated," she added candidly.

"Are you still proofreading James' book? What's it about?" He was making a note to himself in the stenopad.

"With James it's not all that easy to tell."

"Not always, is it?"

"You've read his books?" She seemed embarrassed by her own surprise. "I mean, *all* of them."

"Yes. What's this one about?"

She took a sip of wine and, not looking at him, answered, "Theft and betrayal, I think."

"Really? Can you be more specific?"

"That wouldn't be fair, would it? If you want the plot you should ask the author—since it's not published yet."

Bryce realized he'd just been successfully hedged. He didn't know why that should please him. She was, apparently, anxious to protect James. Was she thinking of all the times James took research a step too far? Or maybe she was just naturally evasive. He was suddenly aware of her looking at him, noticing him in a peculiarly analytical way that made him aware of how little notice she must have taken of him before. So much for my ego, he thought.

"You're probably right," he said. "Now getting back to the birds. To your best recollection no one knew they were here except you and Jon, who had forgotten. And they disappeared sometimes since last Halloween. In other words, almost a year ago."

"This must be very annoying for you. Can I get you something? A drink? Coffee? I'm really very sorry."

"No. Just this." He turned several pages over in his notepad to hide his doodles, then handed it to her. "Draw me a sketch, will you? Of one of these birds. Just a rough one will do."

The sketch was quick, but accurate. Looking at it Bryce thought, What a memory for form. But he said, "I think you should make a trip to the station."

Then, bereft of any of the benefits of swishing, whiffing or oozing, Katharine downed what was left of her Pinot Noir.

"Yes, that's one of them."

At this odd hour the station was as close to deserted as it got—just the women in dispatch, the jailers, an odd deputy or two. The Investigations office had the minimum lighting. The bird sat on a shelf crowded between cans of ninhydrin chemical spray, an empty aquarium and an iron, circa 1956. Katharine touched the tip of the bird's partially opened beak. From Bryce's vantage point it created a strange optical illusion, the bird seemed to be affectionately nibbling her finger.

"I'm so glad you found him. Thank you," she told Bryce, making an unconscious gesture of appreciation by touching him, feather-light, on the arm.

Bryce moved to his desk and, somewhat formally, said, "It was found among Evan Christie's things."

She could not have presented a more sublime picture of apathy.

"There are five in the series, correct? We found . . . only this one. Are they catalogued? Could we possibly get photos of them?"

"Yes, of course. I'll contact my agent." She tentatively asked, "I don't suppose I could take him now, could I?"

"We have to hold onto him a while longer."

"Oh, well," she said, taking a breath. "At least he's safe here. Which is more than I can say for home. Right, Sergeant?"

"It might help if you put them somewhere you can see them."

She laughed. "Maybe."

"A closet seems a strange place to keep something that well done. Why did you?"

She shrugged, smiling the kind of smile that told him she didn't know how to answer the question. "I didn't want to sell them and I didn't want to see them every day."

There was nothing left for them to do. He was going to head to Crystal Bay for bacon and eggs. It crossed his mind to ask her to join him. He even opened his mouth to do so. Then he saw the bird peering at him with a very human eye. It seemed to see something in Bryce that made him laugh.

Katharine and Bryce said good-bye.

Fourteen

Mist blurred the mountains into sky, gave the impression the lake was no longer confined but part of the sea. Katharine parked at a beach and sat in the MG, hungry but not relishing the idea of a meal alone; tired but unable to consider sleep with the sun nearly up; wanting to go to her rooms but realizing that her private place had been violated and now felt strange and dangerous. What she really desired, more than anything, was to be held, to fall asleep with a thick muscular arm sheltering her. Even cry.

She started the car.

James woke with the uneasy sense of something gone wrong. First, there was the matter of his sleeping quarters. Or rather, the fact he wasn't in them but was cramped on a couch sized for a three-year-old child instead of his very comfortable bunk. Also, there was a thin burning sensation dividing the bridge of his nose. The sun was coming through a crack in the curtains. Sleeping here with the sun up seemed an odd thing for him to be doing. Out of the corner of his eye he caught sight of a small bronze bird gazing at him, mouth open, as if about to divulge some good news or, full of perverse cheer, issue a warning. Ah, yes. Kevin had called just before he'd left for the party to tell him he was going to drop this by. Funny of Kevin to have plunked this little gem on his galley table without so much as a note. It was Katharine's, definitely. James wasn't happy about the responsibility of safeguarding this little treasure, even for a day. He intended to give it back to Kevin at the first opportunity. Boy, was Katharine going to be surprised at having one of them recovered so quickly.

The back of James' neck felt suddenly prickly and his stomach sick. Beyond the bird Katharine was standing stock-still in the center of the galley and looked as if she had been rooted there, like Lot's wife, for a very long time.

She was surprised, all right.

"For God's sake, *don't* say anything."

But James felt strongly that he should speak, explain thoroughly the situation at hand, expound upon his innocence. Katharine clamped her hand over his mouth.

"Wait a minute, will you? James, I'm going to make some statements that may seem unrelated, but they aren't, not really. Listen carefully. We've had a good time, haven't we? Nice, easy companionship." As if afraid she might be mistaken, she looked at him. He nodded enthusiastically. "There are certain aspects of your novel," she continued, "that are very similar to some recent events here, is this not true?"

He nodded, markedly less enthusiastic. That's Kevin's fault, he wanted to shout. But her hand still firmly sealed his mouth.

"Now I don't know how you got this—and I don't want to know because that sergeant is a very bright man. I don't want to have to lie to him—for any reason."

James nodded again, miserably. Playing the game by her rules was tricky, but she was trying to make it easy for him. When it was all said and done he knew she would let him go on the technicality that he hadn't directly lied to her. She took her hand from his mouth.

"Did you take this sculpture from me?"

"No."

She pressed her hand against the back of his neck and kissed his forehead roughly.

"You can be an ass sometimes, but you're not stupid, James. And you're not weak. I don't know what you're doing but whatever it is, don't let the same thing happen to you that happened to Evan."

"I won't," he said.

"Shut *up*!"

James took a swallow, like the gulp of a guppy in water. She stuffed her hands in her pockets, bent her head back, exposing the strained muscles of her throat. James felt an unexpected urge to lay his head at that vulnerable spot, stroke her hair, tell her it was going to be all right. But she couldn't stand being lied to; and he didn't know if it was going to be all right or not.

"You should let me explain at least part of it," he said.

She shook her head. "If it's that important it will come out eventually. In the meantime, I don't give a shit."

Yes, of course, he knew that. In contrast to most of the other women he had known, the things he didn't understand about Katharine bothered him less than the things he did.

"Do you want to take him?" He indicated the bird.

She straightened. "No. I was going to give him to you anyway. But be careful, it wouldn't look good if that sergeant found him."

Could Kevin have planned this? James wondered. No. Planned was too strong a word. Hoped against hope was probably more like it. Katharine put her foot on the stairs.

"Where are you going?" he asked, fearing she might leave Tahoe altogether.

She sighed. "I'm going to go to my room and pull the covers over my head." She paused. "Do you have a better suggestion?"

Unfortunately, stupidly, he didn't.

Fifteen

Jon was feeling the uncomfortable prick of dissatisfaction. That new painting of the Swensons' was really nice, he had just the place for it. He really shouldn't consider it. But then again, why not? He liked things tidy but . . . it was unbelievable how readily everyone accepted that Evan had been capable of gaining the necessary information, carefully constructing a plan of action and carrying it out with the proper expertise. It seemed yet another example of how easily people were led, how willingly they left themselves open to disaster. Jon allowed himself a world-weary sigh.

But what about Bryce? Jon had chosen to confide in him because the issue had not been burglary or even art, but power and control. But what good was this power if no one was aware you had it? Of course, everyone knew that he—Jon—was an influence in the community, but no one, he thought, realized the extent. So Jon had conducted his test. He vaguely had to acknowledge that his confession to Bryce had the flavor of a young boy showing off before a man whose hands were tied behind his back. Bryce might caution people not to confide the details of their security systems to anyone, but "anyone" did not include Jon Craig. People approached him asking advice, seeking opinions, to which he always gave a wise and serious consultation. He was their family counselor, their friend. Bryce might be liked, well thought of, but Jon was an old-timer. Bryce would have to be careful how he conducted his investigation. Jon smiled. What Bryce needed was hard physical evidence, and he didn't have any. Nor would he get any.

Katharine was a nuisance. He didn't like her hanging around so long. And she and James were flaunting their relationship like a couple of dogs. James couldn't be blamed. Katharine was hopeless—always had been. Jon had tried hard to do his best by her. Probably something in the genes. She was like her mother—only her mother had been beautiful and Katharine wasn't. Surly, too. Katharine never had shown him the respect he deserved. Apply the right pressure and she would run. Since she'd discovered the birds missing, almost two weeks now, she was in her studio more. Not doing much, he'd snuck in to look. Maybe she and James had had an argument? Maybe James was finally pressing her for some kind of commitment? Poor James. He really didn't know what women were, he put them on a pedestal. And Katharine had such a fickle heart, Jon knew only too well.

It might be a good time to pay James a visit.

James was hunched in the hull, playing with the diesel engine. Jon stood above him in a slightly superior but benevolent position, saying, "She enjoys being mysterious, don't you think?"

"She's always been quiet." James felt disloyal saying even this much. Perhaps because with Jon almost anything you said could be used against you.

Jon laughed a little. "Yes, I suppose you could say she was quiet. Does she talk much to you about her trips to Europe?"

Did she? Yes and no. "Some," he said.

"The people she meets? What she does with her time?"

James remained stubborn. "Some," he repeated.

"You've been friends so long now, but I suppose there are things she doesn't feel free to say, even to you."

How had they gotten onto this subject? James wondered. He should have been paying more attention. But, damn it, the plugs on this thing . . . James was looking at Jon's shoes—the way the leather had been fastidiously shined, the way his feet were planted firmly together like someone's maidenly aunt. He fought an impulse to dribble diesel oil on them.

"A young woman, even more so, an attractive one, living alone, traveling from place to place, she's definitely made her own lifestyle, hasn't she?"

James looked up carefully.

Jon continued: "You know how it is, how women are tested in this world. I wonder how she holds up to it all. Alone. Ever wonder what the reasoning is behind these rapid moves of hers?"

James understood Jon's line of thought. James was angry not because he thought it necessarily untrue but because he didn't feel it was any of Jon's—or his—business.

"I mean, why move, say, even from Tahoe unless you don't feel your activities will hold up to day-to-day scrutiny?"

"Scrutiny or supervision?" James responded, rather proud of the distinction he was making. Jon dismissed this with a shrug.

"It could be construed as free-spirited, I suppose. And Katharine certainly has made it work for her." Jon paused. "Of course, I deal with it constantly in my profession, when I work with women. You know how they are. Never satisfied, always looking for that knight in shining armor—"

James was incredulous. "Katharine's looking for a knight in shining armor?"

Jon was suddenly ambivalent. "So to speak. Artwork has always been first with her. People are secondary."

James was still staring at Jon's shoes.

"The party's tomorrow night. It will be the biggest yet—four hundred or so guests. You're coming, aren't you?"

James said, "I wouldn't miss it for the world."

Sixteen

"Guinevere, aren't you ready yet? Most of the guests have arrived and the band is going to start playing any minute."

Katharine stuffed another tuck of hair into a cone-shaped headdress, then shook out the long gossamer sleeves of her gown. Feeling suitably medieval, she opened her bedroom door.

"And you complain about me," she teased.

"A host should always be available to his guests," Jon said.

"What an excuse to come in a tuxedo while everyone else makes perfect idiots of themselves in costume."

"I'm a maître d'. Very appropriate, I thought."

"I know, I know, I've heard it all before," she said and they laughed. It was an old joke, not so much funny as comforting to Katharine that there was one part of their history they could both enjoy.

Orange and black crepe paper had been twisted around the stair railings, draped from the ceiling to the curtain rods. Dummies had been stuffed and positioned to pop out at the innocent passerby. Rooms were rigged with the supposed sounds of haunting and terror, while jack-o'-lanterns were carved to grin at the chaos with sadistic pleasure. The diningroom table was heavy with food, catered under Claude's supervision: meat trays, elaborately decorated cheese and pâté boards, chaffing dishes filled with meatballs, stuffed mushrooms, and rumaki. Most of the downstairs furniture had been removed to make room for a dance floor. Against one wall a platform had been set up for the band who were now taking up their instruments. They were a motley collection of young people, all dressed in black: two sleazy-looking girls wearing heavy makeup, an alarmingly thin young man and another whose pale blond hair was accentuated by his dark clothing. Katharine stopped to look at him. He was familiar somehow. She was about to ask Jon about him when the lead singer jumped on the platform. His tall lean body was decked out in leopard-printed leather pants that fitted him like a second skin. A mane of tawny hair flowed over his shoulders and curled out of the deeply scooped neck of his leopard-printed tank top.

"My God," she said, distracted, "where did *you* find a group like this?"

"The booking agent got them for me," Jon said, without looking at her. "I don't question my booking agent. I just tell him to get me something good and he always does."

"Well," she said, "the party should be interesting, if nothing else."

"It will be *plenty* else. Excuse me, I'm going to make sure the kids aren't spiking the cider."

Left alone, Katharine wandered through the party looking for James. As far as she could tell through the maze of costumes, he hadn't yet arrived. She went to the buffet, didn't take much of what was there, then wound up throwing the few scraps she did take into the garbage. She visited the bar where she was joined by Laura Parnismus, James' sister-in-law, a former model, now a beautiful face stuck on an ever-thickening body. Ed, her husband, was a corporate executive in San Francisco and they owned a holiday condominium on the lake. She was costumed as a voluptuous Elizabeth I.

"You're looking regal this evening," Katharine told her.

"It's my new image. Stiff collars and propriety."

"That could hide a multitude of sins."

"Hopefully, it will. Say hello to Ed, will you, when you get the chance? He's hiding with Petter in the corner, hoping he won't have to dance. Inga talked Petter into wearing a Swiss hiking outfit—supposed to be a yodeler, I think. See him? He's got very good legs for a man his age.''

Katharine eyed him objectively. Laura babbled brightly on, balancing the handles of four mugs of hot wine between her fingers, as expert as a waitress.

''If you're waiting for your Prince Charming he's going to be a little late tonight.''

''My Prince Charming? You mean James?'' Katharine said, visibly taken back.

Laura smiled and winked and went cheerfully on her way. The lights dimmed and ghosts set on a wire system flew overhead while guests oohed and ahed in unison. Most of them were dancing to the band's eclectic selection of popular songs. A group of teenagers were herded close to the bar, perhaps still in hopes of spiking the cider. One of these youngsters, a boy of about seventeen, caught Katharine's eye. He was smiling eagerly at her and she had the dread realization that at any moment he was going to cross the ten feet between them and ask her to dance. She gulped her drink, did her best to appear six feet tall and hatchet-faced. But obviously precocious, he started to move. Katharine turned, saw Bryce at the bar wearing his usual uniform of jeans and a flannel shirt. She touched his arm and said, ''Help.''

She didn't realize how panicked she must have looked until she saw him adopt what she felt sure was a purely professional expression of concern, saw briefly in his eye an alertness that bordered on excitement.

She pleaded humorously, ''Would you dance with me before that young man asks me and I'm forced to make some lame excuse? Please?''

The band began playing a slow, relatively soft selection. Bryce put his hand on the small of her back and she felt a surge of apprehension, realizing she had just jumped out of the frying pan into the fire. She sounded a little desperate to her own ears when she said, ''I don't dance well. I'm going to step all over your toes.''

''Relax. I can handle the pain.'' And as if he immediately guessed where her problem lay, he said, ''And let *me* lead.''

She looked at him; they were very nearly the same height. And her next question was too near the truth to be completely lighthearted. "How do I know if where you're going to lead me is where I'm going to want to go?"

"It probably isn't. But try not to let that bother you."

As they danced Katharine saw Inga across the room, talking with Martin Anderson. Behind Bryce's back Inga gave her an enthusiastic thumbs-up sign. Katharine put her cheek on the soft flannel covering Bryce's shoulder, determined not to look at Inga anymore.

When the band took a break she went with Bryce to the bar. He gave her a glass of hot wine while he, she noticed, stuck to cider.

Why? she wondered. Is he on duty? Never trust a man who doesn't drink when you do, she had been cautioned by an elderly prostitute she had used as a model a few months before. On the whole she thought it pretty sound advice, though not one she had much occasion to use.

"You know—" Bryce was cut off by a clamor on the patio—people yelling and shrieking, the clink of metal against metal, the high-C whinny of a horse.

"What the hell—?" Jon was suddenly beside her as through the French doors onto the dance floor came a sallow white horse, probably twenty-five, and scarcely alive. Perched precariously on his back was a knight in shop-worn armor.

James was in that twilight zone—not quite rollicking drunk but certainly not sober. He peeked out through his visor as he scattered guests across the dance floor, sent them scurrying ahead like messengers to the dining area. For God's sake, where was Katharine? And where was Jon? He hoped he wasn't going to have to negotiate the stairs. He saw Laura, who gave him an unregal wink and pointed daintily toward the bar. Dear Laura, she knew exactly what he needed to continue this lunacy. Another drink.

But at the bar he saw Kevin on one side, Jon on the other, holding poor Guinevere captive between. Righteously indignant James dug his heels into his ride, babbling some elegant nonsense for all to hear about Lancelot, Camelot, the search for the Holy Grail and the rescue of the queen. He made the horse so nervous it reared. But as James finished he was pleased to hear cheering and applause, to see dimly through the slits Jon radiate a fine purple glow.

James pulled Katharine onto the front of the saddle, and with a flick of the horse's tail, journeyed beyond the French doors into the forest.

"Can we stop now? I'm slipping."

"Unfortunately, this animal is on its way home and I'm not sure I can do anything about it. Unlike me, it has no mouth."

"In another minute I'm going to land on my gossamer rear."

"Don't worry. I'll be right behind you."

They landed, Katharine with a cushioned thud and James with an enormous clatter, in the compost heap of some organic neighbors. Katharine's headdress took a dive into the root of a tree, bounced and rolled into a creek. James lay groaning feebly in the soft compost, his visor popped open to admit its fertile scents. She crawled over to him and cradled his head in her lap.

"Shit," she said.

"Yes, it is," he conceded amiably. "And we're sitting in it."

"Well, little boy Lancelot, there was a reason for this spectacle, I suppose?"

"Jon had a man-to-man talk with me to let me know you were looking for a knight in shining armor. I graciously provided one."

There was an ominous silence. James closed his eyes. His head seemed to reel, then clear, leaving him tired and alcoholically content. Suddenly Katharine started laughing.

"Here comes my knight in shining armor and what does he do? He drops me in a pile of . . . have you ever been kissed while sitting on a heap of rotting vegetables and manure?"

There was a sincere, energetic try on both their parts.

"This isn't working," she said softly.

James sighed. "Discouraging, isn't it? As long as we've known each other, as well as we get along, it would be so convenient."

"But you're a romantic, James, convenience wouldn't satisfy you."

"Would it satisfy *you*?" He felt defensive. He must have sounded it, too. She smiled and Jon's word "mysterious" came back to him. Irritated, he demanded an answer: "Well?"

She kissed him so tenderly he had half an impulse to shout—*I made a mistake*!

She said, "See how wise we are, not to spoil an almost perfect friendship?"

He was skeptical. That second kiss had been a good deal more convincing than the first. He sat up, ready to expose the statement for the evasion it was. But the weight of his suit propelled him too far forward, too fast. His visor plopped down catching part of his lip.

"*James*!"

He lifted the visor, feeling painfully silly. "Laughing is not the most effective way of showing your concern, Katharine."

So she stood and assisted him to his feet. "If I help you hobble home, will I redeem myself?"

He grunted and moved stiffly through the woods, a little lost and foul tempered. She tugged on his arm. "Wrong direction."

"What are those lights then?" But as he spoke the lights went out.

"Probably kids sneaking off to smoke pot or neck," she said. "We're over here."

James saw the glow of the house to the not-so-distant right. He moved slowly in hopes Kevin would spot them on the way in.

* * *

Katharine led them behind the garage to the kitchen in hopes of avoiding Jon. But he was lounging against the kitchen counter, talking with Claude and Ed. He greeted them heartily.

"Well, here they are. Guinevere returning to the fold. A little dirtied in the process."

"We fell in the Fredericksons' compost heap."

Jon smiled eloquently.

James pulled off his helmet, examining the fragrant clumps stuck to the armor. "Show's over for tonight. We obviously can't continue with the party. I suppose we *could*," he said, revising his opinion, "but we won't attract much company."

Katharine watched Jon's eyes go to James' swelling lip. She went to the sink. Taking a wineglass from a rack, she started the tap. Upstairs and out of the way I'll go, she told herself. But Jon was at the sink, whispering in her ear, "If I'd only known it might have been appropriate for me to come as Arthur, don't you think?"

The glass snapped, tearing open her palm. In the first flush of anger she turned and it was only the sight of Bryce coming into the kitchen that made her struggle for control. Jon stood back, his expression roving between satisfaction and something she could not identify.

"Nasty cut," someone said. Everyone seemed to be saying something.

"I should be more careful," she heard herself say. She was handed a towel for the blood.

"How did it happen?"

"It just seemed to pop," she said dully.

"You need a doctor."

"No, really. It will be fine."

"I was just on my way in to say good-night. I could take you by Emergency," Bryce told her.

Claude said, "It looks deep. It might take stitches. And you'll need a shot, considering where you've been."

"I'll have to change," she said, giving in.

"I'll get Laura to help you," Ed told her, and without being too authoritative propelled her on. In a daze she heard James' voice, pert and questioning.

"Just as an historical sidelight, Jon, didn't Guinevere prefer a convent to returning to the fold?"

Seventeen

It took eight stitches to close the wound. She touched it once, fascinated at the weave of black thread and red-lipped scar, before they bandaged it out of sight.

Bryce had been called on an emergency, so it was James, hurriedly pried out of his suit, who waited for her at the hospital.

"One half-hour per stitch," James told her. "They must get paid by the minute. You look like you need a drink."

She did and she didn't. She didn't need the alcohol but she did need the things that went with drinking it: the glass to hold, the rich amber fragrance of cognac, the companionship. Yes, she needed a drink. She nodded.

"Sergeant Bryce called. Asked if we'd drop by a for a drink," James said. "Would you mind?"

"Would you? You don't look excited about the idea."

"I think we should go."

She shrugged. "Well, then. He seems nice," she said, more as a test than an opinion.

"Yes. He used to be."

James knocked once and entered the cabin without waiting for an answer. Bryce was kneeling by the fireplace, coaxing more heat from the coals with a poker. He straightened slowly, and the jovial welcome of a host was absent from his face when he turned. Three small snifters had been set on the walnut table, a jot of brandy in each. Nobody took any and he didn't offer it. James sat on the couch. Katharine took the chair by the brandy. Neither sat back in their seat.

Bryce said, "Inga's dead and it's definitely murder."

"How? *Why*?" asked James.

"The *Lady at Tea*, the new painting, is missing." Bryce rubbed his face as if trying to erase something from his features, then continued on dry, detached. "Inga left the party early, so she may have startled them mid-act. The autopsy report will give us a good idea how long she'd been dead and we can compare that to the time she left the party. I talked to Petter and he said she left right after your performance. Petter said she really enjoyed it . . ."

Katharine took a brandy. She sniffed it, swirled it, watching it go round and round, and never touched it.

"Did she startle them and they hit her—something like that?" James seemed to be pleading for a quick and painless method, almost an accident.

"No," Bryce said, softer than ever. "She was strangled with a cheese wire from her kitchen."

Katharine groaned. James started to go to her, but one look from Byrce set him back in his seat.

"The murderer was very cold-blooded about it—came behind her deliberately. Inga wasn't a small woman. Even though she was sick, it was still no easy job. From the looks of the kitchen she put up a hell of a fight," he said. He went to the table, but instead of taking a brandy he switched on the lamp, spotlighting Katharine. "It was a brutal murder," he said, and adjusted the shade.

"Kevin—" James interjected, but Bryce went on as if he hadn't spoken.

"I wonder if the murderer knew she was dying. If he figured he was doing her a service. Or that murder's not so bad when the victim's got one foot in the grave anyway. Seems hard to imagine someone we know taking that kind of megalomaniac reasoning."

Katharine's eyes were watery. "A lot of people have a surprisingly . . . unorthodox . . . way of reasoning things," she said.

Bryce agreed. "And it's very hard on some of the rest of us. Like Evan."

"Evan?" she questioned, unable to make the connection.

"I think Evan was the victim of some unorthodox methods."

Katharine wondered if this man's voice ever became harsh. It seemed he could make any horrible truth sound like a lullaby.

"That was an accident," she said, but not convincingly.

Bryce went down on one knee, as if proposing, so that he and Katharine were eye to eye. "I have a question for you. Would an outsider have access to the kind of information this person does? What do you think?" But he could no more read an answer on her face than he could reach out and touch her. Here were no written laws, no spoken protests, just a withdrawal he couldn't penetrate. Abruptly, he got up and returned to the fireplace.

"I'm very tired," she told him.

"Yes, I imagine you are."

Her eyes went to Bryce, perhaps to see if she could detect any irony on his face. But his face was protected by an expression of perfect blankness.

"I'll take you home, Kat," James said.

She got up slowly. "I'm sorry," she said to Bryce. "I'm not up to late-night discussions. It all seems to be going over my head."

"I don't think any of us are thinking well at this point."

He went to the table and took a brandy.

When James walked back into the cabin nearly an hour later he found Bryce standing by the now dead fire, studying the ashes, giving the impression he had stood there since they had left without so much as raising his head.

"Do you mind if I ask what you were trying to do, Kevin? You sounded like you were trying to badger her into a confession. I'm telling you, push her too hard and she'll be on the next plane."

"I know."

"She couldn't have done it."

"No."

"Then what—"

"Get her to think," Bryce said quietly. "The first night she was back, when Steve made himself obnoxious at the party, she did something that surprised me. After I got rid of him she asked if I played the piano. That was interesting for two reasons. One, because whether she realized it or not, it was a defensive technique. She wanted the conversation on grounds she knew how to cope with."

"And the second reason?"

Bryce frowned, grinding ash into the stone with his foot. "I asked how she knew and I almost didn't think she was going to be able to tell me. She's intelligent, she's intuitive, but she's not analytical—not unless she has to be. So—" he looked directly at James "—if she isn't involved I want her to think, to use her head. She lives there, she has to know something that will help us. And if she is involved I want her running scared," he finished with exquisite gentleness.

"You can't scare someone who doesn't care, Kevin."

Bryce studied the fireplace ashes again for a few minutes before he spoke.

"Jon is her family and whatever tension there is between them, that may still count for something. Those were her fingerprints in Evan's bedroom, on his closet door. Why would she be in Evan's closet? The sculpture wasn't in there, James."

"Bull. Ask her. There's a reason."

"And I've got news for you, Jim-boy. She does care about something. She cares about you . . ."

James, without having to think, without having to pause, knew where Bryce's thoughts were leading him. He'd known the moment he'd opened his eyes and saw that stupid bird laughing in his face.

"There's another angle to approach this from. If backing her into a corner makes her think, it can be arranged."

"I don't like that idea."

Bryce rested his body against the mantel and tried to say it as nicely as possible. "Tough shit."

Eighteen

Inga Swenson's murder was to change the complexion of life at Lake Tahoe. The most immediate effect was the atmosphere of mourning, for Inga had been much loved. But underlying the mourning was uneasiness. As one matron would state: "I felt much more comfortable about our thief before he took to murder." They had taken the thief for granted, as an accoutrement to having something worth stealing. And no one doubted that it was for her art Inga had been murdered. She was dead and her *Lady at Tea* was missing.

There was a subtle but unmistakeable pressure on Bryce to "do something". Although no one had any more helpful a suggestion than to "arrest the lunatic!" Exactly what lunatic to arrest was left vague. Bryce was supposed to know. One person did suggest an eccentric old man who rambled around King's Beach. And when asked what evidence Bryce had to arrest him on, replied: "Well, he's crazy, isn't he? You never know what a crazy is going to do!"

Bryce found all these suggestions trying.

He spent the day after the murder doing automatically all the things he would normally do in that situation. He rechecked the house, looked over the evidence the staff had accumulated, waited for the autopsy report. He visited Petter in the living room of Laura and Ed's condominium where they were acting as a buffer, taking the many sympathetic phone calls as well as the less sympathetic ones from the press. The room was furnished with expertly crafted log furniture and Navajo wool.

"Petter, you think it was about ten-thirty when Inga left the party?"

"Yes, I believe so."

"You saw her leave—saw her to the car, I mean?"

"No, I met an old friend at the party, so I stayed. I watched her walk to the door." He stopped, folding and unfolding his hands fiercely. "I didn't stay much longer than she. An hour or so. I wasn't even going to stay long. But my friend—we talked—"

Their silence was neither companionable nor awkward. Finally, Bryce said gently, "I'm sorry, Petter. I hate to have to question you now."

"No," he said simply. "Do not distress yourself."

"Petter, can you think of any reason Inga might be murdered other than the obvious one—that she surprised the burglars?"

"Yes, of course I can."

Bryce stared at him in surprise.

"Will you tell me who? And why?"

"It seems very straightforward, does it not? They come, the painting is gone and . . . so is Inga. Very simple, yes?"

"Things aren't always as obvious as they seem."

Petter remained silent, thinking.

"Please," he said, finally. "I will make it more clear later. I don't want to make unreasonable accusations against anyone. Very straightforward, it seems. Yes?"

Bryce was forced to agree.

"Her will," Petter said, more loudly, "will be read here the day after tomorrow. Will you come? Inga had a comfortable income all her own. The reading is at ten."

Bryce nodded. He left, meeting Laura in the hall.

"Are you through with him?" she asked. And though Bryce knew the phrasing was not meant to be unkind, it still annoyed him; as if he thought as little of Petter as a dishtowel, to be used and discarded.

"For now," he said. "I'm glad you're taking care of him. It's too much for someone to be alone when this sort of thing happens."

"Are you going to be handling . . ." She couldn't seem to arrive at the appropriate euphemism, so she left the sentence unfinished.

"It looks like it."

"James has . . . ah . . . told us a lot about you," she said hesitantly, but put her hand to her hair with the smugness of a woman who knew a secret and was glad.

Bryce smiled, embarrassed at his sudden selfconsciousness. To cover it he asked, "Has Jon been by?"

"Yes. Earlier. He said he'd stop by again."

Bryce was about to leave when he noticed how quiet the house was. "Where's Brussels?"

"What?"

"Brussels. The dog."

She looked blank. "I don't know. I haven't seen him."

He forced himself to move unhurried back to the living room. Petter stood uncertainly as Bryce reentered.

"Petter, where's the dog?"

"The dog?"

"Last night. Was the dog home last night?"

"No. Inga took him to the vet yesterday afternoon. He had to spend the night. It was an emergency. A problem with his stomach. Brussels has a bad stomach. I must pick him up today," he finished vaguely.

Closing the door, Bryce looked thoughtful. It was too bad about the dog. No one except Inga and Petter could get into the house without him raising a noise and in that neighborhood the houses were close together. There was one neighbor in particular he irritated with his racket.

"Mourning the absence of your eyewitness, Kevin?" Laura asked quizzically.

Bryce answered drily, "He would have done better under cross-examination than some I've had."

Back at the office, Bryce dialed a New York number.

"Steve, can you do me a favor? Could you gather up any backstreet art gossip about Katharine Craig?"

''Gladly. Is she a serious suspect?'' Steve sounded hopeful.

''You don't like her, do you? Do you know something I don't?''

''Her attitude stinks. If you ask me, she could stand a lot of watching.''

''Well, Steve, we'll do our job. Now, will you do yours?''

Bryce hung up, flagged down the sergeant in charge of patrol just as he passed the door.

''Is Anderson in?''

''Called in sick.''

''Hangover?'' Bryce asked, trying to imagine Anderson drunk. It was nearly impossible.

The big, bald-headed sergeant shrugged. ''Didn't say. If you're in a pinch, call him. Maybe he got lucky last night and is still recovering from the surprise.''

And Bryce thought, Maybe.

Nineteen

It was nearly four o'clock before Katharine woke feeling guilty on the one hand for being in bed so late, and on the other relieved to know much of the day had passed without her. The recollection of the previous night came back to her, bringing a dull ache in her head to match the one in her hand, kindling a sense of dread she did not expect would be easily relieved.

She dressed and went downstairs to face whatever miserable detail might be waiting for her from Jon's quarter. She found him tidying things near the bottom of the stairs, no doubt waiting to intercept her on her way to the kitchen.

"Good morning," she said.

"Good afternoon," he corrected, pointedly.

She hesitated, weighing the merits of each room for a possible conflict. Over the breakfast table? Not very dignified—a disadvantage to have a mouth full of sweet roll. But here and now without the fortification of a cup of coffee? Unthinkable. She went to the kitchen, selected the thickest, heaviest mug from the cabinet and poured coffee. Jon followed her under the pretence of emptying ashtrays into the trash compactor.

"I picked up the mail this morning," he said, "and there's something for you."

A manila envelope was propped on the counter. She had only to look at the return address to know it was the catalog of the bird series.

"Hand hurt?"

"Yes."

His back was to her and she wondered whether he smiled

when she answered. But when he turned his face was full of concern. She automatically raised an eyebrow.

"Are you going to be leaving soon?"

"I haven't made any plans so far."

"You should. It's not safe here when Inga can be murdered in her own kitchen."

Whatever Katharine had expected, it wasn't this. She drank coffee, he washed ashtrays. She managed to say, "Considering my decadent lifestyle, I'm surprised you worry."

"Of course I worry. I've always worried." Righteous and motherly, his chin trembled. "I've done nothing *but* worry."

Cautiously, Katharine moved back a step. Jon took the time to neatly stack ashtrays.

"I'm leaving myself this afternoon. I've got a seminar in Sacramento. I don't think you should stay."

Gathering her patience around her like a protective mantle, she said, "What you're saying is that you want me to leave."

"I don't think it's *wise* for you to stay. I'm only thinking of your welfare. There's really nothing for you here, is there? You don't do much work. There's James, of course, but are you really being fair to him? If you're honest with yourself?"

"If I'm hones—" Hard as she tried she couldn't get the words out. She watched Jon take her hand.

"Believe me for once, Katharine. It's probably best for you to continue your work free of distractions. You do it so well, you know. You've got quite a reputation now. In many ways, I'm so proud."

She stared at her hand in his. Then looked directly at him and said, with unusual finesse, "Go fuck yourself, Jon."

She breakfasted at six-thirty in the evening on linguine and red wine served to her in what was formerly a log post office and now an Italian restaurant. Spread out before her were the five photos from the catalog. It was obvious that

Bryce suspected someone in her intimate circle of not only burglary, but murder. And not the murder of a faraway stranger, but of another intimate. Did she have any information that would help? And if she did, would she turn it over to Bryce? Or did it depend on who it would accuse?

She'd drunk over half the carafe of wine before she came to any conclusions.

Twenty

The MG had limited powers of navigation and the last leg of the road to Bryce's cabin was too much for it. Parking at the bottom of the hill, she walked. A light was on in the cabin and she took heart that this walk in a cold, dark forest, on a rutted road, was not in vain. Tripping, she swore as the jarring brought extra pain to her hand. She hadn't bothered to take the painkillers prescribed.

She tapped on the front door and waited, trembling partly from cold and partly from a contradictory sense of anxiety and anticipation.

He opened the door slowly and looked past her, puzzled. "You walked?"

"MGs were not made to four-wheel around washed-out roads. Is that how you keep out the unwanted? By designing a road like that?"

"I didn't design it."

"You didn't fix it, either."

He smiled. "Come in," he said.

Katharine was struck, as she had not been the night before, by the cabin's blatant masculinity. She turned quickly to Bryce.

"I've got something for you." She gave him the manila envelope.

Removing the photos, he said, "Have a seat."

But she stood by the fireplace, huddling in her sweater, a heavy wool, grey and pink, with a single line of reindeer embroidered across the front. She read the titles of the books on the shelves until she was startled by the whistle of a kettle.

"I was just about to make myself a drink. Would you like one? It'll dull the pain in your hand."

"Please, I don't mean to interrupt whatever you're doing," she said, only to give him an opportunity to get rid of her if he wanted.

"Hot brandy or rum?"

She did not require additional convincing. "Rum," she said.

"You have a lot of books," she said, taking her drink. "Do you really read them or have they just managed to pile up?"

"I read them," he said.

"I used to like to read. I don't much anymore. At least, not fiction."

"No? Why not?"

The question seemed very personal. It would have been easy to say "because I don't have time"—but that seemed such a flimsy excuse and this man was not one to accept an easy answer.

"Because books fiddle too much with your expectations," she told him frankly. "I find a lot of them either too pessimistic or too ready to gloss over the hard part—romanticize—I guess that's the term. And I don't care to be drawn in either way. Does that make sense?"

He nodded, reluctantly.

"I think the ones that romanticize are the worst liars. It would be too easy to want life to be that way. And I don't want to desire anything that has no basis in fact."

"Now *that*," he said, lightly, "is very pessimistic."

"You see? I have enough deep, dark thoughts of my own—I don't need anyone else's."

He smiled and sat in the leather chair. Katharine slid into the far corner of the couch.

"The photos are reasonably good," she said.

He took some time studying them. The last two, she saw, gave him pause. The first three were conventional enough poses. But the last—stretched and pulled to their limits they looked like the victims of a nuclear holocaust. Working her way purposefully through her rum, she wondered what he thought of them.

"Will you need these back?" he asked.

"No."

He looked pleased and crossed his legs in masculine fashion, the ankle bone of one leg propped on the knee of the other. She noticed his socks, extra-thick cotton boot socks dirtied slightly on the bottom in keeping with the pattern of his foot. His jeans were worn nearly white and he had on a soft green pullover, sleeves pushed up to just below his elbows. He looked very much at home there with his drink and his books and odd papers. One hand, muscular and nicked, rested on his thigh and she found herself staring at it.

"What did you enjoy most? Doing this or your *Ball-on-Chain* series?"

She paused long enough for him to realize she was uncomfortable. He laid the photographs aside.

"I had a lot of affection for the bird series so it made the time pass pleasantly. *Ball-on-Chain* came more easily, though. Have you seen *Ball-on-Chain*?"

"No. I know someone who was very impressed by it. I was treated to a whole editorial on the subject."

She raised an eyebrow. "Poor you."

"I have to confess," he said wryly. "Art and emotions have a lot in common. They always sound ridiculous when you talk too much about them."

She held up her glass in a mock toast. "A man after my own heart. What I really hate is answering questions, especially from someone you hardly know. *Tell me, Miss Craig*," she mimicked, "*from where do you draw your inspiration*?"

Bryce looked vaguely horror-stricken. "How do you answer that?"

"I'm usually so tongue-tied they think I've gone into a trance. They like that, really. Think it's artistic, a sudden creative vision or something. Jon thinks I'm being perverse for not baring my soul to the world but . . . I don't know," she finished, suddenly aggravated.

"I don't think you're being perverse," he responded seriously. "I mean, you have energy, you find a way to harness it, to make it work—trying to explain it usually sounds silly, useless or, worse yet, pretentious."

She resisted the impulse to glance at him sharply. With her great respect for privacy she was afraid to look, afraid she might see what was none of her business. For he responded with an understanding she found curious in a policeman. She watched the log become ash and filter through the grate. She watched the shell collapse; small sparks flickered, then drifted dully up the chimney. Bryce got up and put another log on the fire.

"You seem to have some understanding of the system. Too bad you're not an interviewer," she said to his squatting back.

"But I am," he told her without turning. "I just don't interview for the newspaper or television, that's all. Understanding situations has to be a part of my business."

"Sounds logical enough." She did not sound convinced, she realized. Still squatting, poking the fire with a tool, he turned heel enough for her to see his profile, to speak to her with more clarity.

"If I can't understand people and what makes them tick then how can I expect to uncover any kind of truth? That means understanding in spirit what can't be explained precisely in fact."

She admired Bryce. He could say something like that without sounding like an idiot. That took a remarkable balance of sincerity and bullshit.

"What have you been working on, Katharine?"

Her name sounded odd to her coming out of him—the familiar coming out of the unfamiliar. It was like a caress from an unexpected but well-liked source. He did have a lovely voice.

"Nothing."

"Unusual for you, isn't it?"

Like a flash from a lighthouse, a wariness went from her toward him. But he had set himself on the rug, propped back on his elbows, innocuous, unofficial.

"I've suffered from a distinct lack of initiative and have been very easily led astray," she said lightly.

"You don't seem worried."

"I don't worry about my work, I simply do it."

"What do you attribute your 'lack of initiative' to?"

She smiled delicately. Bryce was to remember it as one of the most provoking expressions he had ever encountered in a woman.

"I don't attribute. I don't worry. And if I talk too much I'm liable to sound ridiculous. What do you do in your spare time?"

"I don't have much."

"No? Surely Tahoe isn't as busy as all that. And you've no . . . family obligations. You spend it all reading Proust or Günter Grass?"

"My stepfather was a professor at Stanford. He always encouraged reading. Now it's a bad habit."

"Ah—that explains your reading material. I don't know too many who read Proust or Goethe for pleasure. Or even James. I don't know how his last book became a bestseller, unless it's the jacket cover. Lovely design. Looks elegant on a coffee table." She finished her drink.

"You don't like his books?" Bryce asked quickly.

"Not exactly pulp reading, is it? All those big words and black humor, and for all the sex they're not very erotic," she said, as though this particular conclusion saddened her. "Wonderful imagery, though. And such creative dirty language. Amazing how he can spend four hundred and fifty pages demonstrating the last two paragraphs. I love his books."

He sat up on one side, facing her, and for her part in this *pas de deux* she tucked her feet under her, backing off.

"That's interesting," he said.

"Is it? Does it reveal something terrible in my character?"

He smiled. "I'm going to tell James you said that."

"He'll probably tell you it does."

"Do you think he'll tell me what that terrible something is?"

"He probably doesn't know."

He got on his knees, moved closer to the couch. "That's all right. If there is something terrible, I'll make a point of finding it. Another drink?"

"I think I can handle one more."

Twenty-one

Bryce took his time making the drinks. He wanted a few moments to figure out why Katharine had showed up at his home instead of the office, and to rationalize his own reasons for allowing her to stay. He was pouring hot water into the cups when her voice came from behind him.

"Lovely kitchen. It's so quaint one might be tempted to cook in it."

"It hasn't tempted me so far."

"How long have you been a bachelor, now?"

"To all intents and purposes about four years but, officially, probably not for another month."

"So what have you been doing all that time?"

"There are restaurants, canned soups, and cheese. I can also successfully cook an egg."

"You do better than I do. Although I can make coffee, even the non-instant kind," she countered proudly.

"I'm impressed. My grandmother used to grind her own every morning in this grinder." He briefly touched a blue-and-white tile grinder attached to the counter. "One of the best smells in the world, was her coffee."

Katharine gingerly tested the mechanism. The faint scent of coffee mixed with that of her perfume. She bent low, opened the grinder drawer, and a few strands of hair fell into the plastic container of Tom and Jerry mix. Without thinking, he brushed it back and she straightened quickly.

"Your hair," he explained, "was falling into the rum batter."

"Sorry," she said. She was very close, but made no attempt to move away.

He tilted a few locks of her hair between his fingers saying, "You've got it in your hair." Taking a washcloth from the sink, he moved a fraction closer and in a playful way tried to pass her hair back to her and hand her the cloth. But the bandage on her hand made it awkward and they realized she wasn't going to be able to do it herself. Bryce cleaned her hair. Katharine watched his hands.

"I don't know how but you've got it clear up here," he said, rubbing the line at her temple with the flat of his thumb. She stared up at him.

He thought seriously about kissing her. Unconsciously, even bent his head closer. What actually kept him from doing it, he didn't know. It was possible he didn't like the idea of kissing her one moment and questioning her for murder the next. It was more likely he sensed her stare was not entirely due to any desire for him. He let go of her and stepped back. And if he had any second thoughts they were dismissed by her next words.

"Sergeant, what do you look for in a murderer?"

He took his drink and walked to the door before answering.

"For this one I'm looking for a liar. An exceptional liar. He lies not only by what he says, but by the way he lives."

She picked up her drink and stared inside the glass.

"Tell me," he said quietly, "of all your close circle who do you think would be the most likely murderer?"

"Any one of us, depending on the set of circumstances."

"Even yourself?"

"I said any one of us."

"That's being candid."

"No, it's academic. You're going to make an arrest based on motive and opportunity—and evidence, I assume. Not on theory. So I'm not worried."

"Why do you come and go so much, Katharine?"

"I'm not that fond of Tahoe. The scenery is pretty, but there're a lot of places with pretty scenery. And Jon and I don't really . . . we aren't that compatible."

"But it's not just Tahoe. You don't stay anywhere long."

She said, wryly, "I have a tendency to wander."

He smiled. "Like the children of Israel?"

"On the contrary, it's a very American notion, that we can just leave and make a better life somewhere else—look at the pilgrims."

"Have you made a better life somewhere else?"

"I haven't come across anything worse."

And what astonished Bryce was that she wasn't being flip.

"Any more questions, Sergeant?"

"What did you take out of Evan's closet the night he died?"

"A sweater. I forgot mine and he let me borrow one. It won't do any good to look at me like that. I don't lie."

"No. But you're good at leaving things out."

She pulled her lips together as though trying to suppress a smile. "What exactly are you trying to get from me? Information, or a confession?"

He stayed quiet for a few seconds longer than necessary. The tall woman before him waited with patience, an air of gentleness. They were qualities he used himself, when he thought them necessary. He guessed she could probably match his hardness, too. He braced one hand against the doorcasing.

"I just want you to think, that's all, Katharine. Just think."

She glanced at his hand. She put her drink back down on the counter. She hadn't drunk any of it.

"I haven't been in the woods behind our house for a while, but I did notice something last night with James. There were some lights—like flashlights or maybe headlights—just east of the house, which I think is just empty area. They were on and then suddenly went off. I thought it was kids from the party out doing something they shouldn't."

"Maybe. It's easy for people to come and go in a party

that size. No one ever knows the difference. If you disappear they think you're dancing or got lost on the way to the bar."

"Unless someone happens to be at the right place at the right time?"

Bryce smiled a funny sort of smile. It was an expression she found particularly attractive in him. She said, "Could I ask a favor of you? I know you're busy . . ."

He waited for her to continue but she exhibited a reluctance, as if she just realized what she had said and regretted it. He said, "I'm sure I have an hour or two I could spare. What do you want?"

"Would you come to my studio and pose for me?"

Bryce was stunned. "Pose?" he repeated.

She smiled the same provocative smile she had used earlier. "It's not a dirty word, you know. I promise not to ask you to strip."

Bryce crossed his arms and let out a deep breath. "You mean there's no chance of my becoming an updated version of the statue of David?"

"I did have something else in mind if you're not going to be too disappointed. You'll do it, then?"

"What are you planning to do?"

"Do I ask who you're going to question next or the results of your latest report? It's just a chance you'll have to take."

And, dammit, he *was* curious. In the books he wrote with James he had put himself firmly in an unacknowledged position. So, unlike James, Bryce rarely met anyone in legitimately creative fields. It would be interesting to see how she worked, what her focus might be. Bryce made a quick impulsive decision that, since it put him squarely in the center of attention, went against his grain.

"You can have an hour. Now."

Katharine took three.

Bryce drove Katharine back to her car.

"Next time drive a car that will make it up the road," he said.

The surprise on her face told him she hadn't planned on there ever being a next time.

"Does that mean I'm invited back?" she asked. Forgetting, he supposed, that she hadn't been invited in the first place.

"If you have any information pertinent to the case."

"Oh." She nodded. "What if I need another sitting?"

He shrugged and said as noncommittally as he knew how, "We'll see."

His phone rang as soon as he walked in the door. It was Steve.

"The woman is a dove who rolls in the mud and comes out clean."

"Can you be less rhetorical and more specific?"

"In Paris she's been spending time with prostitutes. In London, a group from a bizarre, drug-orientated club scene. In Greece, a family involved in smuggling. In San Francisco, it's been a certain chain-and-leather element."

"That's a hell of a crowd."

"The prostitutes have a great deal of affection for her, I understand. She does not snort coke in London. The Greeks seem to think she is some kind of Madonna and the San Franciscans think she is very nice. From all appearances she seems more interested in work than debauchery." Steve sounded unconvinced. "She uses all these elements in her work, you know."

"I know."

"There is one other thing you might be interested in. In New York, just before she came to Tahoe, she was walking down Fifth Avenue with Carmella Richards."

Bryce quietly repeated the name.

"Right. One of the women who tried to buy the stuff in Marseilles."

"Do you know this for sure? Who saw them?"

"My secretary. He loves Katharine Craig's work. He's the one who took me to see the *Ball-on-Chain* series I told you about."

"Did he notice the date he saw Katharine?"

"August 29th. The same day he had his wisdom teeth pulled. That's how he remembered. He was on his way to the dentist when he saw them."

There was a long pause on Bryce's end of the line.

"You still there?"

"Let me know if you find anything else, will you, Steve?"

Steve was all too eager to promise.

Twenty-two

"So you weren't surprised by the contents of the will, Petter?"

"No," he told Bryce. "Inga and I had discussed it. Even what charities she would leave money. I am, financially, very comfortable. Inga—and I agreed with her—thought it would be a waste to leave money to someone already wealthy since we had no children. The things she left me were sentimental."

Bryce nodded, admiring these people for doing what some would consider foolish—admiring anyone who put their money where their mouth was.

"Tell me about Inga's brother."

"There is one of Bjorn's type in every family, I suppose—though hopefully not one so extreme. He was older than Inga and had . . ." Petter hesitated on details, paraphrasing them in one word ". . . problems. He left home early and traveled around Europe—even to Asia and South America, we heard. Then before we came to America we got a letter from him. He was in California and had a son."

"And then?"

"Nothing until just before his death about a year ago. We exchanged letters."

"You never looked him up?"

"No, never. He had been very . . ." Petter again had difficulty ". . . much trouble to all the family. And he did terrible things to Inga. They were sexual in nature," he stated primly. "She did not wish him any harm but still she did not care to see him. Nor even his son. That is why we had not tried to communicate with him yet."

"I see. How old would the boy be now?"

"In his early twenties. Bjorn died without any kind of substantial funds so Inga was concerned about him."

"And yet she made that stipulation—"

"Inga was not one to—how is the expression?—throw good money after bad. She did not want to waste money on him if he were like his father."

"So once he is contacted he is to be told very little and then you are to spend a period of time to get to know him and—"

"And I am the one to judge," he said evenly. "If he is satisfactory he will inherit a sizeable amount of money. If not, he will receive a comparatively small lump sum and all monies will revert to the American Cancer Society."

"Unusual."

"Yes." Petter downed the rest of a small vodka. The lake, visible through the windows of the bar, was choppy and the sky overcast. James was sitting at one end of the bar. At the other the bartender was setting up little bowls of lemon and lime pieces, while casually dressed men sat on stools discussing business and laughing. Petter looked at them as if the sound of their laughter were something both foreign and remarkable, though Bryce knew Inga had often made him laugh, right out loud.

Bryce took a firm grip of Petter's hand then released it, surprised at the responding pressure.

"Could the nephew have known about the will?"

"I don't know. The last information we got regarding him was that he was in a foster home in Carmichael about ten years ago."

"That's not far away."

"No. But still, he did not know us. And from what I can gather he was not on good terms with his father."

"His father did have your address up until the time he died, didn't he?"

"True, but the boy never tried to contact us."

A cocktail waitress interrupted them to ask if they wanted something else. They did not.

"Who else knew about the will?"

"Myself, Laura knew—she was a witness, and so was Ed. I discussed it with him. And with Jon Craig. Or rather, Inga talked to Jon about the idea some time ago, asking advice."

"And Jon encouraged the idea?"

Petter gave this question a great deal of thought.

"He did not encourage or discourage. He merely listened, from what I gathered from Inga."

Bryce glanced at his watch.

"What was going to happen to the *Lady at Tea* after Inga's death?"

"It was to be donated to a museum in our hometown in her honor."

Deputy Anderson walked stiffly into the restaurant. Bryce stood.

"Can I drop you off somewhere, Petter?"

"No, no. I am meeting Ed and Laura here for an early supper. They will be here any minute. And James, he will be joining us."

Bryce felt awkward about leaving Petter, though he would soon have company—and good company, at that. Perhaps it was something about the stiff upper lip he didn't quite believe, knowing that dangerous time when grief hasn't yet found a way to express itself. Bryce gave him a gentle pat on the back and said, "Take care."

It was Claude's sudden presence behind the center of the bar, as though timing it for the precise moment Bryce would be available, the busy motions that accomplished no discernible task, the tentative glance in Bryce's direction, that made him walk right up to the bar and say, "Are you ready to talk now?"

Claude dropped a scarcely used towel into the bar sink. "Yes." And both relieved and anxious he began, right where he was, talking low.

"I do not know who Evan was blackmailing, except that it was an affluent member of this community. Evidently what he saw was something from a bedroom, a lady's bedroom, of course. And, gentleman that he was, he did not specify the lady."

"What did he see?"

"Stolen paintings. Evidently, he ran across their temporary storage center."

"Where?"

"He did not say."

Bryce felt half an inclination to reach across the bar and shake Claude. His face must have spoken for itself because Claude hastened to add: "But I have done some thinking on my own. Evan was always working on his house. Though there were few construction workers, there were many deliveries from a moving company. But, alas, I rarely noticed much new furniture."

"What moving company?"

"Sierra Van and Storage. It has a very—" Claude paused delicately over the next word "—small listing in the telephone directory."

"Why now, Claude?"

Claude reached behind the counter and gave a swift jerk of his head. Bryce turned to see Petter staring out the window at the billows of white clouds with black underlining. James had joined him, but his attention was elsewhere. Bryce saw James' face turn serious, then surprised. Just then Bryce was shoved to the side, saw out of the corner of his eye Claude lifted over the counter, thrown to the floor and, in one well-synchronized motion, kicked solidly in the balls. A towel fluttered to the ground a few feet away. Gasping, Claude folded into the fetal position. Anderson, the initiator of these violent proceedings, fell on him, pulling Claude's hands from his groin. Claude's small tight fists could not have been hiding anything more bulky than a hairpin but still Anderson pried them open with the skill and speed of an oysterman shucking oysters. Once proved empty, Anderson got up and stumbled to the bar.

Bryce knelt to attend to Claude. The bartender, full of concern, leaned over the bar, one hand searching for a brandy bottle. The two businessmen stayed in their corner, peanut-filled mouths open wide. Petter looked on without interest. Only James, perhaps because he was the only one left and because, also, Anderson had caught his eye from the moment he'd walked in, rushed to the scene.

Anderson half rested on a stool, small pools of moisture in the pits on his face.

The young man refused to meet Bryce's eyes. Perhaps, thought Bryce, I don't appear sympathetic. That wasn't surprising. He wasn't.

"So what you're saying," Bryce articulated carefully, "is that when you saw me look away and Claude reach down behind the counter you thought he intended to do me some bodily harm. To what purpose, with at least five eyewitnesses present? And why, since we have no reason to, or intention of, arresting him at this point?"

"I don't know, sir. It was just an instinct."

"An instinct," Bryce repeated doubtfully. Anderson's eyes flickered. Bryce tapped a pencil against Claude's desk. "This isn't the first time you've jumped the gun, is it, Anderson?"

Anderson remained silent.

"You aren't with Los Angeles County anymore. We do things differently here, we have a different rapport with the community. There's a lot of money here and money doesn't like having its nuts shoved up its throat on account of obscure instincts."

Anderson presented no argument. Bryce suddenly asked, "Were you with the crew that checked the forest east of the Craig home today?"

"Yes."

"What did you find?"

"There were tire marks in an area just inside the National Forest where the ground is soft. We took casts. There's an overgrown path from an old fire road that meets the path between the Craig neighbourhood and the Swenson residence."

"What kind of vehicle are the tire marks from?"

"A van of some kind."

"Any footprints?"

"Looks like about a size ten man's print. Clean soles, no treads. Might have been a brand-new pair of something like a gymnastic shoe."

"Anything else?"

"No. The site was really clean except for a rusted can of Orange Crush and an empty matchbook."

"From where?"

"Here." The "sir" was conspicuously absent. Anderson was unusually white. Bryce preferred it when a person flushed red rather than drained white when angry. Something about the bloodless angle disturbed him.

"That's not very conclusive," Bryce stated patiently. "That's not even probable cause."

Anderson refused to either argue or concede. He shifted in his seat rather painfully.

The last thing Bryce wanted was to tie another policeman's hands, make him overly cautious about applying physical force. God knows, he had been physical often enough himself. But perhaps what disturbed him most about Anderson was not his action, but his attitude.

"Get the hell out of here, Anderson."

Anderson's startlingly blue eyes grew wide. "Does that mean I'm suspended?"

"You bet your ass."

Anderson rose slowly, moved awkwardly out the door as if his whole body were slightly out of balance. Bryce wondered what exactly the illness was that had kept him out for a day.

After his exit there was a tentative knock on the door and James appeared, resplendent in white cotton trousers and a textured navy-blue sweater under which the collar of a pale-blue Oxford shirt inched up just the appropriate space. James' hands lounged carelessly in his pockets. And, in defiance of the notion that the casual handsomeness was too studied, there was a small smear of what appeared to be mustard above his knee, a scab from shaving on his right jaw. Bryce looked at him as if he were seeing him for the first time through different—perhaps more feminine—eyes.

"How's Claude?" Bryce asked.

"Like the ministering angel I am, I've given him a substantial dose of brandy. He is now half crocked and nearly painless. And between bartender George and I, we've managed to shove his balls back down his throat to where they belong." James sprawled onto a chair. "You don't look happy."

"No."

"What was he doing?"

"Protecting me from whatever Claude was reaching for behind the counter."

"But he was getting a towel."

"Correct."

"What was he doing here?"

"He'd been out with Browning and Browning told him I wanted to talk to him. He was driving by, saw my car and stopped in."

"He couldn't have waited to see you in the office?"

Bryce let out a deep breath.

"That's one heck of a guardian angel you have—"

Bryce looked at him sharply.

"—because I'm telling you, Kevin, I was watching that guy—watching his face—and he liked doing that to Claude. He *enjoys* giving pain."

But Bryce had known that all along.

Bryce stopped by the office. Browning was sitting with his feet on his desk, flipping through the autopsy report.

"Death by strangulation," Browning drawled. "The cheese wire was definitely the instrument. I tell you one thing—she put up a hell of a fight. Whoever did it must have been one strong son of a bitch. Another thing you might be interested in, Kevin. Coroner seems to think she might have done some damage to him."

"What kind of damage?"

"Reconstructing the action from the marks on her, he

seems to think she must have caught him hard somewhere on the lower leg. The ankle, maybe. Then they both went down. That position finished her—even if he was hurt he had the advantage then. He must have been like I said, one strong son of a bitch. Of course,'' he said getting up, tossing the report on Bryce's desk, ''I could be full of shit. Got a football pool going. You want to join in? 49ers look hot.''

''No, thanks, Barrett. Next time, maybe.''

Detective Barrett Browning shrugged. ''Well, when you've got such sophisticated taste in art, I guess football pools don't sound so exciting.'' He grinned and slung his jacket over his shoulder, ready to call it a day.

Bryce smiled faintly.

Somewhere in the lower leg . . . the ankle, maybe . . . One strong son of a bitch . . . the ankle . . .

Jon had looked fine. Was it possible for him to have escaped the party long enough to commit the crime? Maybe. Probably not. But could Jon have an accomplice? Bryce hoped if he did, whoever it was was someone from Sierra Van and Storage. It would make life so much simpler.

Bryce found the listing and drove to King's Beach where the address was located one half-mile off the main highway, on the outskirts of the barrio. The building itself was mainly a garage with an apartment to the side, built of wood, old but in good repair. There were some newer storage cubicles at the back. It appeared to be locked and deserted. Bryce peered in a window and saw what he would expect to see in a garage: tools, grease stains, magnetic signs stacked against the wall bearing the company logo, dollies and blankets. Bryce knocked on the apartment door and though he knocked loudly and long there was no answer. At a break in the living-room curtains Bryce could see a snatch of nice modern furniture, a sophisticated stereo unit, a poster on the wall of the rock group Bon Jovi. At the kitchen window he could see crumbs on the table, a plate and two mugs in the sink, a frying pan soaking on the stove. There was a loaf of bread on top of the refrigerator. Abandoned, thought Bryce, but only temporarily.

Bryce walked the grounds. There were no immediate neighbors, but up behind, rising over the tops of the trees, was a small cluster of townhouses. Bryce went back to his car and checked his notes.

He'd bet anything Patricia Truscoe was living in one of those townhouses.

She did. And she wasn't home, either. But Bryce was fairly sure her townhouse provided the appropriate view. He only wanted to know if Patricia could provide any more appropriate information.

He'd stop back later.

He went back by Sierra Van and Storage. Still nobody there.

And on that exquisitely frustrating note, he went to see Katharine Craig.

Twenty-three

Katharine had worked all day, using as her resource the drawings she had done the night before. The sergeant had surprised her—all those stationery supplies. Most people on instant notice would be reduced to the backs of envelopes or inadequate sheets of letter stationery. But right there in a kitchen closet he had the most magnificent array of supplies—even colored pencils, had she desired them. She couldn't help wondering what he did with all that paper, those pens, typewriter ribbon, and, good God, six boxes of correctional tape? She hadn't seen a typewriter. Where did he keep it and what did he type on it? She tried to imagine his fingers on keys and while at first the picture seemed incongruous she was sure they wouldn't be anything less than accurate.

Katharine stopped working just after dark, went out and grabbed a small meal at Claude's with James for company, though he'd already eaten.

"You've got clay in your hair and you forgot to wash your face," he told her.

It was true. She'd been absent-minded. And her hand, which she'd managed to work around all day, and seemed to be healing fast, was now throbbing a little. At the moment nothing sounded more desirable than to be in bed between soft flannel sheets, hugging a feather pillow.

It seemed strange to see the sergeant's car in the driveway. Not because she didn't expect him, for she had in a way. Maybe not this evening, but soon. No, it just seemed odd whenever his world and Jon's crossed paths. In contrast to Jon, the sergeant was refreshingly earthy, *wholesome*. She was glad he had come. Had she analyzed this she might have found it an unusual attitude to take toward someone investigating herself and her close associates for murder. But she didn't stop to analyze. She hurried inside enjoying the sense of expectation, satisfied to see her basic conviction upheld by the fact Bryce didn't wait for her in one of the more traditional rooms, but had gone ahead to her studio. The door was open and she saw him sitting against the window, tapping one of her pencils on the sill, before he saw her.

"You're very official-looking this evening, Sergeant," she said by way of greeting. And the slow, deliberate way he stood and took his time answering, the way he held his shoulders unconsciously a little stiffer told her the reason he looked official was because the visit was official.

"I have to ask you some questions," he said.

By the time she walked through the door and sat against the worktable she had made the necessary change from anticipation to formality.

"Are you acquainted with Carmella Richards?" he asked.

"The collector? We've met at various functions."

"When was the last time you saw her?"

Katharine gave the question some thought.

"In August, I think. I'm not sure. In New York."

"It was August 29th. Or did you see her more than once?"

"No. If you say it was the 29th then it must have been the 29th."

"What did you discuss?"

Again, she had to think before answering.

"The Roithko exhibit at the Met. Some Danish ballet dancer she had staying with her. And her new grandson—he was born on Mothers' Day."

"Is that all?"

"The weather."

He didn't raise his voice but she knew he was angry.

"Did you know Carmella Richards was planning a trip to Marseilles not long after you met in New York?"

"She didn't mention it."

"Didn't she? She bought a Dove, a Marin, and a Kahlo, all taken from Tahoe residences."

The stillness between them was a living thing; had it been a color it would have swirled bright blue and vivid green.

"Just because I happened to visit the same country she did doesn't mean I had anything to do with her buying them." She pushed away from the table. Her disappointment was more than that of a keenly anticipated pleasure spoiled. It was a throwback, associated dimly in her emotions with past disappointments, when an ally was shown to be an enemy, a source of both pain and humiliation. She wanted to scream, yet when she spoke it was as controlled as ever. "What would my motive be? Let's see." She started pacing. "How about money? Have you seen how much my work goes for? I don't come cheap and I don't spend much. I travel, but I don't worry about going first class."

"You don't worry about the company you keep, either. I'd hate to have any of them swear to my character in court. Wouldn't hold up well," he shot back and she stared at him. "I don't think money would be much of a temptation for you, anyway. But how about excitement?"

"Knowing the company I keep, as you put it, I should think I'd be getting plenty of excitement."

"Ah, but in reality you've been a very good girl, haven't you?"

That shut her up for a matter of seconds. "Maybe I've never found anything worth being bad over," she said, finally.

"Have you found anything worth being bad over now, Katharine?"

She had no answer to give him.

"Let's get back to the night Evan died. You said you went to his home, at his request, to view a sculpture and borrow a sweater, correct? Yet, no one saw him at the party, which means he would have had to come, basically on the sly, specifically for you. What was the reason? Why would he be afraid of being seen? Is it possible you went to his home for an entirely different purpose than the one you told me?''

''No, it's not possible. I said I went there for a sweater and that's what I got. Do you want to see it?'' Without waiting for a reply, she flung open the door to the adjoining bedroom and went for it. She returned, throwing it in his face.

He drew it away slowly and asked, ''Does it have his name on it?''

''His name on it? What is this—summer camp?''

''It doesn't mean anything, you know. You could have just taken it—to cover bloodstains on your dress, for instance. When do you expect Jon?''

''I don't. He said he was leaving town for a counseling seminar.''

''So you were with James this evening?''

She hesitated before answering a small, ''Yes.''

''How did he appear?''

''What do you mean?''

''I got the autopsy report on Inga. It seems she might have done some damage to her assailant. A good crack in the lower limb—the ankle, for instance. James looked fine when I saw him but sometimes it takes a few hours for these things to show.''

''It would have been difficult to wrestle Inga in that suit of armor—''

''It comes off easily with a little help,'' he interrupted her brutally. ''It came from a costume rental in Reno. And you two did take a long time getting back to the party.''

''Would you like a detailed account of what went on while we were away?''

''Would you mind my taking it down word for word and signing a statement?''

''Do you have a pen on you or should I go get one?'' she retorted heatedly.

Bryce rested against the wall. His temper was getting the better of him and taking an account of her time with James, he realized, would only aggravate him further. Katharine retreated to the opposing corner of the room.

"I've told you the truth," she said, more gently.

"I don't," he answered, "suspect you of lying."

She looked at him, more sorrowful than angry.

"Is James back on his boat now?" he asked.

"Yes."

Bryce moved out of his corner.

"Are you going to arrest him?" she asked quickly and he stopped to answer her.

"It depends on what he says and on what I find. I have a search warrant," he lied. "Maybe you should come with me in case there's anything to identify."

She came out of her corner to meet him.

"Why are you doing this? If you build a case against him that means I was an accomplice in Inga's murder. But if you don't think I'm lying then you know you're arresting someone innocent—*why*?"

"To get the guilty party. The only way I can get to him is to use you. And the only way I can get to you is to use James." He took her shoulders in his hands and it took visible effort to keep from shaking her. "I'm telling you this honestly because I want you to understand what I'm doing. You won't look at this on your own, Katharine, you don't want to. But you have to understand that I have no choice but to *force* it out of you any way I can. I know who did the burglaries—he told me, for Christ's sake—but I didn't have any evidence. Now two people are dead and I still don't have any evidence."

If there was one thing she knew well, one thing she really sympathized with, it was the frustration of not being able to control events and results; she'd felt the irrational guilt. And maybe it was because she was used to expressing herself with her hands that she reached up and touched his face; softly, at first, to test his response. Then with more confidence she took the tip of her finger and, guiding his chin closer, kissed him.

A small signal went off in the back of his mind when he laid her out on the table. Not that she wasn't willing but there was something just a little ill at ease about the look in her eye. So he changed his course of action, let her take him to the adjoining bedroom where a second signal went up as they were getting undressed—or rather, as he was getting undressed because she hesitated, watching him. Which he found disconcerting until he caught on to exactly how she was watching, and how that made him feel. Still, it took a sharp, curious look from him before she finished taking her sweater off; and when she did he thought (though technically it wasn't true) that he'd never seen anyone more beautiful and surprised himself by saying so.

She seemed more at ease then, eager to let him help her out of the rest of her clothes.

In his enthusiasm he completely ignored signal number three.

Not until she flinched under him, jumped as abruptly as if she'd been jolted by a shock of electricity did he put two and two together—the uneasiness, the hesitation, the slight initial awkwardness about where and how to touch him, the apparent pain—

"You've never done this before have you."

It was important to him that he keep holding because if she usually appeared a little older than her years, vulnerability now made her a good ten years younger. He knew already she was a woman who really took pleasure in being held, even now kept her arms tangled up with his.

"Did I hurt you?"

"No . . . it just . . . surprised me, that's all."

Jesus, you're not the only one, he thought.

He brushed the hair away from her face. Her ears were pierced with discreet gold balls and he carefully removed them, set them on the nightstand.

"Look, we'll start again and go slower, OK? I'll try to be more gentle."

He felt her thighs tightened around his waist. Her voice was surprisingly strong. "You don't have to be," she said.

But he did have to. And he was.

Twenty-four

A blue jay screeched outside the window. One small ray of sun was baking him through the glass, keeping him groggy and content. He opened his eyes and saw the earrings on the nightstand were gone, felt beside him an empty space. He rolled over and sighed into the pillow, listening for the sound of the shower running, for the jingle of hangers, even the sleek rub of fabric drawn over skin. But there was nothing but the irritating noise of the jay. He got out of bed and dressed quickly. He was still tucking in his shirt as he passed the studio door.

"You're too late."

He walked in slowly and tried to make his face blank and impartial. He did not quite succeed.

She was dressed in the clothes from the night before, sitting in a chair with her feet propped on the worktable. She was drinking a cup of coffee.

"I went to him early this morning. The bird is at the bottom of the lake." She paused before resuming their conversation on a more conventional note. "Would you like a cup of coffee? The water is hot."

He answered her by making it. *Refusing it might indicate a lack of good sportsmanship*, he thought drily. And then, *You have been incredibly stupid*.

He found her looking at him. She cocked her head to one side and said, "You haven't been completely stupid." He sat on the table without responding.

She said, "At least, no more stupid than I've been. If I'd let James explain why he had the bird I like to believe he would have told me the truth—or something near to it.

I'm supposing this sculpture was originally found with the one I identified in your office. And I believe the truth is that you planted it on James' boat in hopes that it would make me think he was involved in some way or that he was in danger. The logic being that when the time came to make an arrest—or fake an arrest—if I knew anything that would keep him out of jail I'd come out with it and maybe then you'd be able to pin the crime on the real criminal. My loyalty seems to me to be an odd thing for you to have put such confidence in, Sergeant. But you were right. James has been my friend for a long time and I do love him. This seems to me to be unusual police procedure."

He said, "You didn't have to throw your sculpture away."

"Yes, I realize that now. When I woke up this morning I wasn't at all certain you wouldn't put James in jail if you thought it would suit your purpose. That's why I was going to get rid of it. You couldn't use it against him if it wasn't there. But I couldn't very well bring it home, could I? That would have been a complication I could do without. I don't know how much official sanction you had for what you did, or if you even needed any, but if I had to explain to someone other than you where it came from—I mean, I couldn't say I'd made a mistake and it hadn't been stolen after all. I'm not a good liar . . . but then I saw how upset James was when he guessed what I was up to. He was yelling at me from the dock saying, among other things, 'it's evidence, goddammit.' And it dawned on me that James had never been in any danger of being arrested. That despite his sometimes screwy approach to researching his books he'd probably never been involved in anything illegal. That the information he was using for his book he might easily have gotten if he had a friend in the Sheriff's department. That the most reasonable explanation was that he'd been cooperating with you all along.

"Would it make sense to you if I said I threw the bird away because at that moment I hated the sight of it? Have I made life more complicated for you, Sergeant? Was that bird to be eventually returned to the station? If it comes down to it, I don't suppose either one of us wants to have to explain last night to your captain."

"I didn't intend to blackmail you into bed," he told her.

"No. I like to imagine that was unexpected," she answered thoughtfully. "You only wanted to get my attention. Well, you succeeded." She paused to drink more coffee. She appeared to be measuring her next words carefully. "I did appreciate your honesty last night—thinking back on it, you didn't have to tell me you were only using James to put pressure on me. Most people aren't honest about ruthlessness. You are a sonofabitch, Sergeant, and I'd hate you for that if it wasn't for one thing. I think, in this instance, you were right. You had a job to do and you did it using the most effective means available to you. You have a murderer to catch and I will cooperate with you."

"Then we have to talk," he said.

"I don't like to talk," she confessed. She sat up, putting her feet on the floor. She looked tired. "I know I'll have to open my mouth sometime but not this morning. I'm not up to it. You trusted me last night or you wouldn't have been asleep this morning—not the way you were. I know I must not make sense to you, but trust me to help, because I will."

I must be out of my mind, he thought, because in some screwball kind of logic I do trust her. But he said, "I don't suppose at this point I have much choice."

She smiled. "You look like hell. Do you want a shower?"

"If I go in looking too bad it's not good for my solid officer of the law image."

She laughed and seemed much more at ease than she'd been a moment before. "Use the bathroom in my bedroom. Everything you'll need is in the linen closet. Even razors."

"I don't want to be accused of rummaging through your closets," he said as a poor joke and, evidently happy for any kind of levity, she took him up on it.

"You've rummaged through everything else, I don't

know why I should get defensive over my closets at this point."

He grinned. Had their situation been touched with less uncertainty and awkwardness he would have picked her up and taken her into the shower with him. As it was he went alone to a bathroom that smelled of something sweet and French and clean—like she had, like even the bed had. He checked the name of the bottles of scent on the vanity surrounding the sink while he dried himself.

She did not appear to have moved since he left but he knew she must have because on the table was a plate with pastry. She had put one on a napkin, but he didn't think she'd eaten any of it—just torn it apart.

"Do you want something to eat?"

"No, I'm late as it is. My phone's probably ringing off the hook."

She nodded, biting her lower lip.

"How are you?" he couldn't help asking.

"Fine," she said, but she took on the reserve he identified with her when she was unhappy or on her guard.

"The only place private enough for us to talk is my home. The place is usually unlocked so you can get in any time."

"I'll make myself right at home."

He hesitated. There was amusement, even kindness in his eyes and, peeking in somewhere between, the faintest trace of bitterness. "Katharine . . . I don't expect a repeat of last night."

"That's very comforting, Sergeant," she stated flatly.

Damn her, does she have to call me Sergeant?

"You do understand what I want, don't you?"

"Of course," she said. "You want my husband."

Twenty-five

Bryce's phone buzzed and he picked up the line.

"A James Parnismus to see you." There was a nervous catch in the young clerk's usually businesslike voice.

Bryce sat completely motionless.

"Sergeant? He seems very anxious—" And filtering in behind the woman's hesitancy was a distinctly male "*Dammit*!"

"Send him up," Bryce said.

James was up the stairs and through dispatch, loudly and within seconds. Bryce was in the office alone.

"Kevin, I've had one helluva morning. I've been trying to get a hold of you since six-thirty. I tell you my life's been so exciting lately I haven't had to manufacture anything. Katharine came pounding on the hatch at five this morning looking like she'd been out all night with a wild man and asked for the bird."

"And you gave it to her?"

"Kevin, I was half asleep—it never occurred to me—she had the rubber dinghy, said 'Sorry, love,' kissed my cheek and *took* it. Out in the dinghy. Into the water. While I stood on deck in my robe like—well, it didn't do anything for my self-respect, I tell you."

Bryce looked at him with more interest. "She didn't explain?"

"To use one of your own lovely phrases, Kevin, she didn't say shit. Just ploinked that bird in the water like it was a snail."

Bryce slowly covered his mouth with his hand.

"I tried looking for it but the water must be hundreds of feet deep there. I wound up tooling around for hours to no purpose." James paused, as if suddenly discovering something both remarkable and irritating. "For losing not only evidence but a nice bit of artwork you don't seem very concerned."

"I'm concerned," he deadpanned.

James rolled his eyes. "I guess I've been dancing on my tiptoes all morning for my health."

"I've got another problem this morning. The autopsy report seems to indicate that Inga might have hurt her attacker in the struggle—knowing how Inga was, probably by accident, tripping over the rug. There was a lot of broken crockery, also blood on a couple of shards that turned out not to be Inga's."

"Except for a slight case of apoplexy, Jon seemed fine the night of the party."

Bryce shook his head. "From the technical report it looks like her attacker limped away."

"An accomplice then?"

"Maybe." Bryce frowned. "I have a lead in that direction."

"Painful things, sprains. Is that what made your deputy so cranky?"

"What do you mean?"

"I mean, he had his ankle taped with an ace bandage. He was leaning against the bar—you had your back to him—but I was on the other side of Claude. The way the deputy was leaning made his pants hike up. I saw his left leg."

Bryce was quiet. "Doesn't necessarily mean anything," he said.

"Well, it means something to me. I don't like the way he cracks people in the nuts, he's sadistic about it." James stood.

"Where are you going?"

"I'm leaving so you can pull his file. You won't do it with me here—not when it involves police 'family'."

Bryce frowned. "You're jumping to a lot of conclusions on no evidence."

"I don't need evidence—I'm a civilian with imagination. Besides, I know a loony tune when I see one. So do you. Is that why you keep him around you so much, to keep an eye on him?"

"You're worse than a wife."

"You bet. I have no physical compensations. And speaking of conclusions with no evidence, I have a question for you. I've been doing some calculations—"

Uh-oh, thought Bryce, here it comes.

"—You asked me to keep Katharine around before the party, therefore before Jon's little announcement. Did you suspect something all along?"

Bryce gave his attention to the report on his desk.

"Let me ask you a question. Do you love her?"

"Of course, in my own—"

"I mean, do you want to marry her? Do you want her to have your babies? That kind of bullshit."

James looked at him as if he were crazy. "Is this rele—"

"Yes."

"No."

Bryce continued perusing the report. James remained where he was, bewildered by Bryce's slightly disapproving manner, sidetracked from his original question.

"Do you object?" he inquired.

Bryce raised his eyes from the report. "No," he said, "I have no objections at all."

His phone rang.

The garage door at Sierra Van and Storage was open and the noisy clank of metal tools falling on a concrete floor greeted Bryce as he strolled in. The van was parked inside and two feet were sticking out from under the back bumper.

"Hello," Bryce called.

A young man rolled out from under the van on a wheeled board. He was about twenty years old with pale blond hair he jammed back with filthy fingers. He looked familiar, but Bryce wasn't sure if it was because he had seen him before or if it was because he so exemplified a type. Blond, permanently suntanned, at the station he would have fitted their definition of the all-American boy: good-looking, IQ of ninety, and still a virgin.

Bryce smiled, taking a friendly approach. "My name is Kevin Bryce. And you are?"

"Andy. Andy Silva." He was wiping his hands with a dirty rag.

"Are you in charge?"

"I'm the only one here right now," he said nervously. "It's—it's my dad's business. But he's on vacation right now."

"Oh? When will he be back?"

"In a month." Andy shuffled his feet and rubbed his hands more energetically. "Maybe more," he added.

"And he left you to take care of business? He must think you're a very capable young man," Bryce commented kindly.

"I guess," Andy said uncertainly, and then asserted with more confidence: "November is a slow month."

"Not much business, is there?"

"No," he said quickly. "Not much."

Bryce looked at him thoughtfully and suddenly changed his mind about his course of action.

"If I needed to have something moved, would you be able to do it for me? This week?"

Andy stuffed the rag in the pocket of his overalls and rolled his eyes, undecided.

"It's nothing big, just a couple of things I don't have time to deal with. If your old man's not around maybe you could earn a little extra cash," Bryce suggested and winked.

The young man shook his head but it was a gesture without conviction. "I don't think so."

Bryce took out his wallet and thumbed through some bills. Fortunately, he had a large one. He took it out.

"It's a very special job," he said. The young man eyed

the bill. "I'm getting a divorce and have a couple of things I'd prefer my wife didn't find. If your dad's not around—" Bryce shrugged "—it would give you something to do."

The boy slowly brightened.

Bryce tucked the bill back into his wallet. "I'll stop by tomorrow. Thanks."

The door to Patricia Truscoe's townhouse was opened by a large hairy man who looked, with the possible exception of all that dark hair, like a young professional. He wore a Hawaiian shirt whose tag must have scratched his neck, for he kept making a kind of rolling motion with his shoulder.

"Looking for Pat, eh?" he said.

"Yes. This is her place, isn't it?" questioned Bryce.

"Yeah, but she's gone."

"Gone?"

"Sublet it to me last week, furniture and all. Haven't been here long. Just opened my practice down at the professional center in Tahoe City. I'm a dentist." He flashed a smile of perfectly even white teeth.

"I see. Had you known Pat long?"

"About four weeks, I guess. Nice lady. Are you an old friend of hers?"

"I'm with the Placer County Sheriff's department. Do you know where she went?"

The man looked suddenly a little worried, rolling his shoulders.

"Hawaii, I think."

"You don't have her address?"

"Paid in advance. And she didn't seem worried about what happened to the place—emergency-wise, I mean."

"When did she leave?"

"The day I took the place. A week ago Monday, I think. She was real nice—real nice."

"Did she say when she planned on coming back?"

"January, I think. Said she needed a long rest."

Or a long distance between herself and Tahoe, Bryce thought.

The man was looking at him with the same anxiousness to please as a big Labrador. "She looked like she needed a rest," he said.

"Would it be possible for me to take a look out of the bedroom window?"

"This way, this way," he said and showed him through the townhouse, which was furnished with the same sort of white modernity that graced Evan's house. There was a telescope at the window, pointed toward the lake. Or rather, as Bryce discovered looking through it, at the window of a condo near the shore. The man behind him coughed. Bryce altered the position of the scope and found Sierra Van and Storage.

Bryce pulled out one of his cards and gave it to the man, requesting pleasantly that he "Give a call, if you hear from her, please." The man seemed relieved. "And your name?"

"Bob. Bob Ridenaur," he said heartily. "Always willing to cooperate with the police. New in town, you know." He pulled out his wallet and from it took a card and handed it to Bryce: Robert R. Ridenaur, DDS. It gave his phone number at the bottom.

"If you need any dental work, give me a call."

"Thanks," Bryce said, marveling at the promotional instincts of the rising young professional.

Bryce went immediately back to his office and assigned to his other two detectives the surveillance of Andy Silva. He briefly considered having Katharine watched, too. It wouldn't surprise him if she went to the airport rather than his home. But what would he say to the surveillance team? Report back if she shows up at my cabin?

No.

Twenty-six

Perched at her draftman's desk Katharine was unable to concentrate. She thought of everything—and nothing coherently. She wanted to work and found herself staring at empty pages. She didn't want to work; doodled rather than sketched and felt guilty because she was wasting time. She threw a pencil across the room for the sheer joy of watching it bounce off the wall. Then got up and went to the kitchen, hungry but irritated that bodily demands went on no matter what else was happening. She found a beer and a box of chocolates and was systematically working her way through both when the phone rang. It was the vet's office, telling her Jon's cat was ready.

"Ready? Ready for what?"

"To be picked up," said a testy female voice. "She was hit by a car Saturday afternoon. We've stitched her up and shot her full of antibiotics. At Jon's insistence she's going to die at home—but don't tell him I said that."

She wrote a note to Jon concerning the cat. Took what was left of the beer and a last Bordeaux cream and started back to her studio. In the living room, dead center, she stopped. She couldn't immediately pinpoint what was different, and even once she realized what it was, could not have listed the furniture missing. She only knew that not everything that had been removed for the party had been replaced. Jon was usually meticulous about putting things back in order. Maybe Inga's death had thrown him, though she hadn't ever noticed tragedy getting in the way of Jon's routine before. Tragedy itself seemed routine to him.

She climbed the stairs slowly, hesitating outside her studio door, and soon found herself approaching Jon's room. Caution made her knock. He *said* he was going to Sacramento; but his words meant nothing. She opened the door and went in, wincing at the claret-colored decor, the harem-like mosquito netting draped over the bed. A grandfather clock was ticking loudly against the silence. And next to it, hidden by a poorly painted lake scene—God, how archaic a hiding place!—was a safe. In all probability Jon had changed the lock. Or, if she was lucky, he considered her with his usual arrogance incapable of remembering the combination. It did take two tries, but due less to her not recalling the numbers properly than to her trembling, knowing she'd have a helluva time getting out of this if Jon walked in.

There were a lot of papers, and some jewelry wrapped in velvet that had been her mother's. She thumbed through the papers: wills, insurance, quite ordinary things. The deed to the house. The deed to . . . another house. She examined this more carefully. Although she was no longer privy to any of Jon's confidences (not that she'd ever had access to them all) it was unusual that he shouldn't mention such a large purchase. The house was apparently located off of Highway 89, in Plumas County. The last thing in the pile was a plain white envelope. The gummed edge was tucked in and, unfolding it, she saw it contained photographs. She tried to look without actually touching them, shaking the envelope to let the pictures fall forward, one by one. *Jesus*, she thought. The clock's sullen ticking was making her stomach tight. She looked at the deed again. A pencil, she needed a pencil. She glanced around the room. Why was it there was never a pencil when you needed one? She was seized with an unreasonable compulsion to hurry. Next to the bed was a nightstand; on it a lamp, some books she knew Jon never read, a Waterford crystal glass and carafe. She opened the drawer and her mother's face stared up at her out of an opulent art nouveau frame, surrounded by odd momentos: an empty bottle of Nina Ricci's *L'Air du Temps*, some hairpins, a favorite scarf, an enameled comb and brush still threaded with hair. She closed the drawer quickly.

Leaving the safe open, the deed on a chair, the beer on the floor, she stuck the envelope of photos in the back pocket of her jeans and closed the door to Jon's room. She walked quickly, not quite running, to her studio where she looked for the pencil she'd bounced off the wall. She couldn't find it. At her desk she got another, brand new and unsharpened. *Where the hell was the sharpener*? And though the clock was down the hall she still imagined she heard it, urging her on. The sharpener was in the back of a drawer. She crossed the room, leaving a trail of shavings as she went. Once back at Jon's safe she penciled the real-estate data on the envelope with the photos and returned those to her pocket, the deed to its proper place. She picked up the beer and went back to the studio, emptying the bottle in one big gulp. She stood there for a long time, staring at the clay studies on the table. And perhaps in an unconscious attempt to distance herself from what she'd just done, she began fingering them, righting a few wrongs. Her smock was soon clay-streaked, her hands dirty. At one point she suddenly realized three hours had passed, that it was growing dark. She went to the sink, soaped vigorously all the way to the elbows, scraped under the nails with a small file.

"Trying to get *clean*, Katharine?"

She recognized the tone and felt sick.

"Just finished for the day, Jon," she said, keeping one eye on him and one on what she was doing.

"Oh? And what are you going to be doing this evening?" he asked with phony civility.

She grabbed a towel and began to dry herself. "I was thinking of going out."

"Oh?" He strolled around the table, examining the models as if taking a deeply professional interest.

"Didn't expect you back so soon." She swallowed, trying to make what was dry, wet. He stopped at the last study and she eased forward like one would to a sick animal that had to be restrained.

"This is interesting. Don't remember you doing anything quite like it before. Is that what last night was all about?

Doing research? Or perhaps James just isn't enough for you.'' Face twitching, his hand in a fist so tight it shook, he raised his arm.

''*Don't*!'' She nearly flew across the table. The fist changed course, catching her just below the cheekbone.

''*Slut*!''

Katharine touched her face and felt tears sprung from some emotionless leak, a biological statement of protest.

''Like your mother. I tried to save you from that,'' he muttered bitterly.

She stared at her saved model, breathing heavily. ''Thanks, Jon. You have a way of highlighting the great moments of my life.''

He slapped her this time. She let him, deciding it was the only way for them to say good-bye properly. He left the house. She washed her face in cold water and went to her room to pack.

Twenty-seven

Bryce made a phone call to Auburn and watched the clock. He'd wanted to be home before now. It felt peculiar knowing there was someone waiting. That is, if there *was* someone waiting. Browning was ironing an envelope as carefully as if it had been his best shirt, to hurry ninhydrin spray into highlighting fingerprints.

"Barrett, why is it you're the first on the computer and yet still use outdated methods like that for fingerprints?"

"Just a complicated guy, Kevin. An old-fashioned man with new-age skills. A Renaissance redneck."

"Is that it? Well, why don't you run the name Andrew Silva through the computer and see what you find? He's about twenty or twenty-one years old."

"Sure thing."

Personnel in Auburn was on the line. Bryce consulted with them, talking low. He toyed with a stun gun confiscated some months before from a convicted rapist who claimed, like some latter-day Robin Hood, only to have it in order to rob a drug peddler. The gun was shaped much like one of Bryce's typewriter cartridges, though a little longer and narrower, and had a switch on the side. He flicked it and watched a sizzle of blue light run between two prongs. He switched it off and kept talking.

By the time Bryce hung up, Detective Browning had his information organized.

"Arrested for grand theft auto about three years ago and was put on probation. Been pretty clean since then except for a speeding ticket. Found a mug shot of him." Browning laid the computer readout and the mug shot on Bryce's desk.

The big, bald-headed patrol sergeant came in, introducing a visiting deputy from Contra-Costa County.

"Browning. Barrett Browning," Barrett drawled. "Like the poet. She was my great aunt."

The deputy, who didn't know who the poet was, looked blank. The sergeant said, "I'm so frigging *sick* of that story."

Detective Barrett Browning grinned and winked.

Bryce showed the sergeant the mug shot.

"Know him?"

"I've seen him. King's Beach boy. Doesn't cause any trouble." The sergeant stated this fact as if it were immediate grounds for suspicion, as if the young man simply hadn't put his cards on the table yet. "I've seen him work around town—the grocery, a gas station here or there. Always near the barrio area."

"We've got him under surveillance right now."

"We'll keep that in mind."

Bryce read the report on the Silva arrest. A high-speed chase had ensued through Tahoe City. Spotted by the highway patrol for making an illegal turn, they had tried to stop him for a simple traffic violation. But he took off, careening through residential areas, scattering flocks of tourists like so many sheep. The chase had ended when the Trans Am he was driving made contact with a classic '57 Chevrolet convertible, parked just the other side of Fanny Bridge.

The owner of the car had been Jon Craig.

Bryce made one last phone call to New York.

Twenty-eight

Bryce drove home quickly, even absently running Tahoe City's one red light. As the last quarter-mile of his driveway bounced him around he thought of having it fixed—not too well—just smooth it out some. His lights illuminated the trunk of the MG Katharine drove. Jesus, he thought, she got that up the hill. She must have been very determined. (She had, in fact, been very determined; bouncing from bump to bump, sailing over the ruts in between.) A white cloth was hanging from the trunk.

The stun gun, which had sat on his desk for so long, was now sitting on his car seat; unconsciously he'd walked out of the station still playing with it. He picked it up and got out of the car to open the trunk of the MG. It contained two poorly packed suitcases and an overnight bag, their zippers unzipped, and contents strewn. He pushed a pair of panties back inside and closed the trunk, considering what this might mean. He checked the inside of the car. The bench seat seemed full of plastic. He picked through the tangle, though the bulb in the car lamp was dim—battery probably giving out—and it was awkward with so little light. When he was able to get his hand inside he felt soft clay. He closed the plastic again.

The house was dark, a fire had been started but was running low. Some latent suspicions—long experience with domestic situations had taught him loyalties could often be misplaced and peculiar—made him enter cautiously. But he could see nothing out of the ordinary in the room's shadows. All the fireplace tools were there and the same logs, minus the two in the fire, he had set out the morning before. He went to the fire and saw her, face down, on the sofa. She'd helped herself to a glass of wine. Her car keys were on the table, her shoes jumbled on top of one another on the floor nearby. It was a condition he found reassuring. Reassuring to *what*? he asked himself and made an inward shrug in reply.

He got the fire going again, but she didn't stir. He went to the kitchen for a drink and set the stun gun on the table. He put on water for a hot brandy, made as much racket as possible getting out the cup and spoon, and half accidently, half on purpose, kicked a kitchen chair, letting it fall with a clatter. After a few minutes the kettle whistled and he let it go on for a bit before he made the drink for which he had little desire. He just wanted something to hold in his hand.

He sat in the leather chair and watched her, struck by how completely still she lay. Not like the night before when she had struggled in her sleep for a firmer hold and muttered short incomprehensible messages.

"Oh, no," he groaned and felt his insides plummet. He was up in a second, at her side; taking her shoulders in his hands he swung her head up from where it rested on her arms. Her face was swollen and touched faintly with blue; the half-opened eyes showed confusion, bewilderment, and finally, irritation.

She rolled on her back and rubbed her face with her arm. She said hoarsely, "There are better ways of waking, people, Sergeant."

"Sorry," he said, but he was smiling.

Moving took an awful lot of effort. She stretched, keeping her eyes closed. She didn't think he'd touch her, but he did. He lifted her arm from her face. She waited for him to kiss her, but even though she knew her perception of time must be out of focus she realized, as the moments dragged on, that wasn't what he intended.

"What happened to your face?" he asked softly.

Always softly, she thought. But it had too much of an edge to be a lover's voice. *What did happen to my face?*

She couldn't remember. Something unpleasant, she was sure, because it hurt.

"Katharine, what happened to your face?" He was insistent.

"I did not," she said tiredly, "have a good day."

"What *happened*?"

"I don't think Jon approves of my sleeping with the local sheriff, particularly under his own roof. He doesn't mind so much the Greek fishermen or Israeli soldiers he imagines I bed down with because they're far away—but things like that shouldn't happen in his Tahoe paradise," she concluded sadly. She expected him to move away and he did. Opening her eyes she saw he sat by the sofa, on the floor, his hands in his hair.

"I am so sorry."

"For what? For going to bed with me? Or for my hand getting slapped when it was found in the cookie jar?" Her words were irreverent, but they couldn't completely disguise a brittleness. She expected an answer. He lifted his head and preserved the silence a little longer.

"For getting punished."

She chuckled deep down in her throat. Slowly, painfully, she propped herself on her elbows.

"I don't know how he knew. He didn't go to Sacramento, obviously."

Bryce got up and took a copy of the Silva photo out of his wallet.

"Is he familiar at all?"

Katharine took the copy and frowned.

"He works for a moving company. Sierra Van and Storage."

"I've never had anything to move but I know I've seen him. Does he do anything besides move things?"

"He's had odd jobs around the lake. He doesn't appear very intelligent. Brawn and no brain."

"Sounds just like Jon's type," she said.

"What do you mean?"

"Jon's kids—you know what he is to kids—they used

always to be hanging around; even his best friends when he was young, his favorites, were always brawny and brainless. That's why James was such a disappointment to him, you know. James is actually very intelligent, though he hides it well."

Bryce smiled ruefully. "He works on cars. At least, he was working on the moving van," he said, taking the picture.

"On *cars*?" She took the picture again and studied it. "What did his hands look like?"

"Filthy. Full of grease."

Into her mind flashed an image of grubby fingers stabbed into pale hair. Unconsciously, she imitated the gesture.

"I saw him at Inga's the day you were there—after you left. He delivered the wrong groceries to her house." She handed the picture to Bryce.

"What store was he from?"

"I don't know. It wasn't a printed order sheet. I've seen him somewhere else, too. I'm not sure where. But I remember thinking about his dirty nails that day, and how he probably had to work on cars to get them that dirty."

"It's interesting but it doesn't prove anything," he said.

Like my life, she thought.

"Can you ever remember seeing him with Jon?"

"No," she said uncertainly. Her hand went to her back pocket, came away again empty.

"What were the circumstances the last time you saw the bird series? What were you holding back?"

"At last year's Halloween party, I was getting restless and snuck upstairs to the studio. I got the birds out, for no reason, really, just to look. Evan must have followed me. He was drunk—you have to give him credit, it takes a lot of ingenuity to get drunk at one of Jon's parties; he's got an eagle eye for that type of thing. He doesn't approve of the excess. Evan was, well, being more friendly than I felt comfortable with." She wrinkled her nose. "I took care of it—to be honest, more abruptly than I usually do. That stupid party always puts me in a bad mood. Jon walked in and felt duty-bound to rescue me in the most obnoxious way, even though Evan and I had already—anyway, I left the party and went to a bar with James.''

''And Evan saw the birds?''

''He'd have to have been a moron not to. They were sitting right there on the table.''

He was silent, thinking. She was observing him with new eyes: the expression on his face, the way he held himself, the way he wore his clothes. She felt an absurd sense of pride in knowing what was beneath those clothes, perhaps having some idea of what might be behind the expression on his face. Though there were things about him that, to her mind, didn't add up. She wondered if she was being a fool.

''Did Jon murder Evan and Inga?''

He looked as if he were deciding whether to tell her the truth. He said, ''I believe he murdered Evan. I'm not sure about Inga.''

She didn't question him. If he really wanted her to know he would probably tell her. And as her silence persisted there was something like gratitude in his eye. Perhaps if she'd asked he would have told her, and been sorry. She reached to her back pocket, brought out the envelope and handed it to him.

''I took it out of Jon's safe this afternoon. I wrote the things on the envelope—it's the parcel number of a piece of property I didn't know he owned. It seemed odd, his not telling me. And those pictures, I don't recognize the house, although I recognize some of the works in it.''

''Katharine,'' he said, ''I didn't know you and Jon were married. Legally, I can't ask you to cooperate in this way.''

''But you can take what's given voluntarily, can't you? And, as you've pointed out before, if questioned I'm very good at leaving things out if I feel it's necessary.''

He stared at her for a second, then balanced the envelope so he could see the pictures without handling them. ''Have you touched these?'' he asked.

''No.'' She paused. ''Will they prove something?''

"They'll help," he said. "It's more than I've got."

Katharine's mind drifted back to her last morning with Inga. It had been perfect, a morning of clumsiness and comedy and warmth that had been Inga's gift to the world. Only Inga could produce a chain of events like the one that had sent her dog into such a frenzy.

"Yappy little beast . . ."

"What?"

"That terrier of Inga's," she said, more loudly. "Noisy, aggressive little thing. I'm surprised he didn't do damage to whoever it was."

"He wasn't there. He was at the vet's."

"He was in good company. So was Jon's cat. She was hit by a car Saturday afternoon," she said.

So serious was his expression, she wondered if he'd grown suddenly angry. "It would be interesting to check the vet's appointment schedule," he said.

"So it would." This is like connecting those dotted line puzzles we had as children, she thought. We can connect number twenty-four to number twenty-five, or number fourteen to number fifteen, but can't seem to align number one with number two. We get a few scattered dashes, but no cohesive picture. "To catch a thief or a murderer he has to make mistakes. Correct?"

"Correct."

"Jon doesn't make mistakes."

Bryce opened his mouth, ready to make a protest, then closed it, waiting to see how she would continue.

"Except in one thing. His choice in love has always been dreadful. So is his way of handling the emotion. Otherwise he's very clever."

He stared at her and she thought he was deciphering what she said. Instead, he seemed to be deciphering her.

"Do you ever speak bluntly?" And when she didn't answer, he said, "He married you."

"Not out of love—at least, not the conventional kind."

"Did you know that before you married him?"

She looked away, sliding her feet against the sofa cushions.

"Yes . . . and no." She paused. "I was too young, too naïve to understand the kind of problems he has." Then, "He was very attached to my mother."

"Why did you do it?" he asked and something in his voice—perhaps it was sympathy, perhaps it was sorrow—made her look at him and look away again.

"I was weak." *How's that for bluntness*? she challenged him silently. "He likes to influence, to have people lean on him. I expected something different than what I got and found I stood better teetering on one foot than leaning on him. Besides, at eighteen you do stupid things."

"Why didn't you get a divorce or annulment? It would have been easy."

"There seemed no point. After the very first night I didn't consider the marriage binding and not starting any proceedings made it seem as if it hadn't really happened. He was . . ." Her face hardened except for the left corner of her mouth, which trembled. She faltered on any more explicit comment. ". . . very unkind," she said. And if she'd ventured a look would have seen Bryce made both curious and truly angry. What had Jon done to her, what had Jon *said*? But he was too wise to ask. She continued on only half aware of what she was saying. "Sex would have been easy enough to get, I suppose, but seemed like more trouble than it wasn't worth. Falling in love seemed to take a kind of trust I wasn't capable of anymore, so I didn't worry about wanting to marry again."

"Why in hell did you crawl into bed so willingly with me?" he asked wonderingly. But that question was even less wise than the other.

Her head snapped up. "Why did you *crawl*, as you put it, so willingly in with me? Doesn't seem smart from your point of view. Especially on an official visit."

"It wasn't. But I did it anyway and I have a reason for it."

Bartering with me, Sergeant? she questioned by raising

an eyebrow. *You tell me yours and I'll tell you mine*? She felt perverse.

"The obvious answer is that I didn't want James put in jeopardy and that I didn't want to collaborate with you because you had something hanging over my head."

"You're being evasive, Katharine." He looked like he was enjoying a joke on someone. On her. Or on himself. "Never mind. We've strayed from the point."

"So we have. I'd like to offer you a piece of advice."

"Which is?"

"Try using the same technique on Jon that you used on me and you might have a great deal of success."

Bryce picked up his drink, rubbing his thumb around the rim of the glass, lightly dipping his finger into the now cold brandy.

"Three years ago the boy at the storage company stole a car and led the police on a merry chase through Tahoe City before he plowed into the side of your cousin's classic '57 Chevy," he said, as if beginning a story he expected her to finish.

"Did he? Was he injured? The boy, I mean."

"He was in the hospital."

"Jon might have visited him. It's the type of thing he would do. He's a memorable person, makes friends wherever he goes. Someone at the hospital is bound to remember him."

"I'll see what I can find out in the morning."

They became quiet. She swung her legs off the sofa.

"Where are you staying tonight?" he asked.

"I thought I'd check into a motel."

"It's after midnight."

"Is it?" she said, as though going from place to place looking for a vacancy and getting an unhappy motel manager out of bed, the probable speculation caused by her bruised face, was an inevitable burden to be accepted.

"I'm sure Ed and Laura wouldn't mind your staying with them. Even James has extra bunks," he said.

"I'd rather not," she said, bending her head, digging her

toes into the rug. Jon had humiliated her all those years before and now Bryce was throwing her out into the cold. Her vision of the rug was blurred.

"You can stay here."

She bent further, grabbed one of her shoes but she had difficulty getting it on. It twisted and turned and the back kept jamming into the sole. He took hold of her unbandaged fingers with one hand, tossed her shoe aside with the other.

"Bathroom's this way," he said, pulling her up. "I'll get your bags and even let you have the bedroom. Just let me wander through for a shower, OK?"

She allowed herself to be escorted upstairs, and washed, while he fetched her bags. She examined her face in the mirror, deciding it didn't look bad, exactly—just less symmetrical.

Bryce soaped himself using the same force he would have used sandpapering a piece of rough wood. He lathered his hair and in his enthusiasm got it in his eyes. He swore, opened the shower door to get a towel, and felt the softness of one pressed into his hands. He dried his eyes. Water was running out onto the floor from the shower's flow. She was leaning against the door in her bathrobe. Lacking any trace of shyness she examined him, at once serious and teasing.

"I don't want your bedroom if you're not going to be in it," she said. She turned but he was too quick for her, catching her wrist.

"*Dammit*, Katharine," he said and pulled her into the shower with him.

Twenty-nine

Bryce groaned into the telephone receiver.

"Wake up! It's six o'clock your time. You should be up by now."

"I have a very good reason for staying asleep," he said roughly.

"Don't we all?"

Bryce was trying to keep from waking up any more than was absolutely necessary. Her back was curled against his front and where he was was a very pleasant place to be.

"Well, if you can hold off being so damned pleased with yourself why don't you tell me why you called so I can go back to sleep?"

"Grumpy, grumpy," Steve said lightly. "I'm in San Francisco with the painting you asked for. I'll be driving up later today and I'll stop in Auburn and get that packet from the guy in personnel. Don't worry, I'll be discreet. Just make sure the painting doesn't disappear."

"It won't. Anything else?"

"About Katharine Craig—"

Bryce rolled away from his comfortable position.

"—I don't know much more than the last time I talked with you. She camped around with the Israeli Army for a while sketching for an exhibit that didn't pan out."

Katharine whimpered and rolled over, laying her body half on his, bumping the phone with her shoulder, jostling it into his chin.

"I'll talk to you later," Bryce said.

"But—"

Bryce hung up and maneuvered her body to lie, warm

and relaxed, on top of his. She mumbled a ''good morning'' into his neck. He ran his hands up and down her back, over the curve of her rear for some time before he spoke.

''Katharine, all this spontaneous sex has been nice but, if we're going to continue with it, one of us better start using birth control. We might already be too late.''

''People have children out of wedlock all the time and it's expected of artists. It's a testament to our wild, unbridled way of life,'' she said, and lay there so quietly Bryce thought she might have fallen back to sleep. But suddenly she asked, ''Do you have any children?''

''A son.''

He could feel the surprise in her body; stiffening it where before it had been soft.

''How old is he?''

He paused for a minute. ''Twenty-four.''

''Twenty-four,'' she whispered and propped her head on one hand. ''How old are you?''

After another, longer pause, he said, ''Thirty-nine.''

''Good God.'' She fingered his fine, thin hair and grinned, hugely. ''Is that why you brought up birth control? Once burned, twice shy?''

It was his turn to grin. He pulled her down into his chest, so she wouldn't see. ''Becoming a father at fifteen made a big impression on me,'' he said.

''I bet,'' she answered and refused to be kept down. ''You still see him? You're close?''

''He was more or less raised by my parents. He's a remarkable guy. Finished college at eighteen. He's an art historian. Also, he works as an adviser to the FBI on art.''

Her stomach was growling, he could feel it rumbling against his. She kissed him. She did it very well, really. He could state without reservation that in the past two days she had made outstanding progress. It was too bad they'd just been discussing fatherhood. He said, ''When was the last time you had a meal? Why don't I make you some breakfast?''

* * *

A sizzling hickory aroma filled the kitchen. Her bathrobe was still soaked and she came into the kitchen wearing her jeans and the shirt he'd worn the night before, though she had plenty of her own.

"I'm adding something new to my eggs routine," he said. "This bacon's been in the freezer for years."

She popped her head over his shoulder. "I guess that makes it my turn tonight. Bring home some steaks. That shouldn't be too hard, should it? You just throw them on the grill and hope for the best. Right?"

Bring it *home*? he repeated to himself. Damned confident, wasn't she? He grinned.

"We'll find out. Try this," he said, handing her a strip of bacon.

Still chewing, she said, "Not bad. When's breakfast?"

"Now." He dished it up while she hugged him from behind.

"Have you ever been to Europe, Sergeant?"

He didn't know why that question gave him pause. Some small warning signal, not unlike the ones he failed to heed their first night in bed, went off in the back of his mind.

"No."

Perhaps sensing some difference, she moved away from him. And before he'd finished dishing up the second plate he heard a sizzle of a different kind. He turned and said, "*Jesus*! Be careful with that thing."

Wide-eyed, she said, "Just wondering what it was."

He put the plates on the table, took the gun from her hand. "It's a stun gun. Do you have to finger everything?"

She made a small, graceful movement with her shoulders. "You didn't seem to mind last night."

"That may be true. But I won't hurt you." He was immediately conscious of an embarrassment, as if he'd just told a ridiculous lie. To make it worse, she was looking at him with one eye, as if she'd spotted the prevarication.

She said, "What does it do?"

"When the batteries are good it can knock you off your feet. As old as these are it would be useful mostly for the element of surprise, which is its main purpose anyway—to catch a person off-guard so you can handcuff them. If you needed to use this you'd go for bare skin preferably, or the least clothed area, for maximum effect, then shove the prongs into it and flick the switch." Bryce had the uncomfortable feeling he was hiding behind technical information. "Leave it on long enough—and even with low batteries that's not long—and you'll burn the skin. Lesson over. Now shut up and eat your breakfast."

She obeyed, dipping her bacon in the yolk of her eggs, ignoring the toast, fidgeting her feet under the table. He thought, She's got more twists and turns than is going to be easy and she enjoys playing games. But so do I, to be honest.

"Do you think you'd marry again, Sergeant?"

"Not if you don't learn my name," he said bluntly and was surprised to see her blush.

"I wasn't necessarily thinking of myself," she said.

"In academic terms, then? No." He softened that somewhat harsh declaration by smiling ruefully. She was fingering the gun again. He half wondered if she was going to use it on him.

She said, "Seems like a real handy thing to have around."

Thirty

"He's taking Highway 89?"

"Yeah. Went through Truckee and just crossed over Highway 80." Browning's voice coming over the radio crackled into anonymity. "Got in touch with Plumas County and they're going to stake out that property you mentioned. Mutt and Jeff are on his trail. I'm working on the search warrant now."

"Good. I'll be catching up to them."

Using his official status he dashed through the lonely traffic of a November weekday. From the moment he'd received the call telling him Andrew Silva was on his way out of town he'd felt an urgency.

"He's driving fast. Seventy-five or eighty," said another voice on the radio.

Good, Bryce thought. Keep it moving, kid. Keep it moving fast. Bryce wondered if there was a special rush or if it was just the natural exuberance of a young man who liked to drive fast.

Did you kill Inga? I have no doubts about your relationship to Jon: part papa and part something you probably don't even understand. It fits; slips into the slot neatly, unquestionably. You're a brawny kid, there wouldn't necessarily be a trace of a limp now. Did Inga catch you in the act of stealing the picture for Jon? Bryce hoped so. With all his heart.

And Jon. Not one to let opportunity pass you by, are you? How lucky for you that your cat strayed under the tire of a car and you found out all would be quiet on the Swenson home front. Such a convenient night—Inga and Petter gone, the confusion of the party. Opportunity on a silver platter. Like Evan.

Always thought somebody's husband would get him, a man remarked to me.

Well, somebody's husband did get him.

You must have been exceptionally rude to Evan, to get him that angry. So angry that one night, perhaps awake with postcoital insomnia, playing with the telescope, he spots you with the kid, probably loading an odd package furtively, curiously. He might have followed you then, or perhaps later. No doubt expecting something more lurid he found your little hideaway, took his pictures. No wonder you were cringing—to be outdone by someone as simple and foolish as Evan, Bryce thought grimly. But he was still afraid of you. He must have been to approach Katharine on the sly. To no use, though. You keep too close a watch on her. And that was the final straw, wasn't it? There didn't seem to be much of a struggle. Maybe it was the last thing Evan expected, Jon, especially in his semi-drunken state—for you to use your hands instead of your mouth.

"He's turning off the main highway," said a voice in staccato.

"I've almost caught up with you."

The county he was racing through was ranching country. High mountain pastures, now gold in color, dotted with white-faced cattle, fenced in by pine forests and barbed wire. Every few miles a farmhouse and barns, tractors and hay bales tall as skyscrapers stood out, lonely bastions of rural civilization. Bryce turned off the highway, winding around a road even narrower and less tended than the main one. Bryce was met by a Plumas County patrolman.

"He's up in that house. You can see it through the trees there. Your surveillance team has staked itself out behind it."

The house was a gracious farmhouse, Victorian, peeking coyly over the tops of the trees. Bryce got on the radio.

"Barrett, how's the search warrant coming?"

"I'm trying to track down the judge. He was last seen

at the Old Post Office restaurant, having breakfast. He's on his way to King's Beach to play golf by now, I expect."

Bryce's response was dry. "Terrific." He thought for a moment, then said, "Let's do a telephonic search warrant. I don't want this kid to leave the house."

Browning said, "My, my, my, aren't things getting exciting? Will do."

They were parked behind a patch of pine and white-barked aspen trees whose leaves shimmered yellow in the breeze. Bryce stood next to the patrolman without speaking, putting more energy into standing still than he would have pacing. It was a lesson in control, a counterpart to the restless boredom of waiting.

A voice over a hand radio said, "He's out the door. Looks like he's getting ready to leave."

"Oh, no, he doesn't." Bryce got into his car, shoved it into gear and took off up the road.

Andrew Silva was at the door, arms loaded not with art, but with personal things: a pair of Levis, a couple of records, a ghetto-blaster. As Bryce drove into the yard, he stopped and looked uncertain, confused. But when Bryce stepped out of the car, his face moved from confusion to recognition. Bryce's blazer was unmarked, he didn't wear a uniform, had never identified to Andy his line of work, but the knowledge was smeared across Andy's expression. A loyal little boy. He'd talked to Jon.

The house had a grand wrap-around porch and Bryce headed toward it as if sure of his welcome. "Hello," he said. "Packing up to go somewhere?"

Andy opened his mouth, then closed it and showed the whites of his eyes. Behind him were a brand-new pair of double doors, freshly varnished, a view of Lake Tahoe carved deeply in the grain. They stood wide open and Bryce could see past the entry into a dining room as big as a mess hall. It held a table in keeping with Jon's delusions of grandeur and on its walls, hung in crowded art gallery fashion, he could see a Constable, a piece of a Bierstadt and the foot of a reclining nude. Propped against a mahogany wainscot, staring gravely, her permanent place as yet undecided, was the *Lady at Tea*.

Elation. It was an emotion Bryce had experienced rarely. It visited him now, gave him a grin and a wink that was a perfect imitation of Barrett Browning. But this warm mimic was lost on Andy who nervously, clumsily, dropped his load, and reached behind to slam the doors. Too late.

"Really nice house you've got. Is this your dad's, too? Looks like it has some unique furnishings."

"You can't get in. You need a search warrant." Andy had probably watched hundreds of police programs on television for he spoke with the authority of an expert. Bryce smiled, kicked a pebble off the porch.

"Sure," he said, "I know that."

Bryce's easiness threw him. Andy stared, shuffled, and swallowed. He bent stiffly to gather his things. A record slipped from its jacket as he went for the Levis, the Levis fell as he tried to catch the disc, the disc bounced down the stairs like a runaway wheel. He kicked the ghetto-blaster with one foot, knocking it over, and with the other crushed another record. Bryce watched this with polite fascination; the Nordic blondness, the virtuoso awkwardness fanning a small, far-fetched hope that what he might be witnessing was a problem of heredity rather than anxiety. Inga, who would not throw good money after bad, would be unlikely to leave anything to a nephew caught burglarizing her household. Jon knew the details of the will, and it wouldn't be out of the question for him to pass them on. And this conclusion would be so lovely, so simple, so much less trouble.

Andy seemed to have arrived at a decision. He drew himself to his full height, ignoring with dignity the debris dropped at his feet. "I'm getting the hell out of here," he said, striding past Bryce.

Bryce said, "Let's talk a little about your driving."

"My *what*—?"

"You were clocked at eighty-five mph on your way up here, and there's a patrolman at the end of the drive who's real concerned about those kinds of speeds—"

Bryce was interrupted by his radio. And once on it Browning said, "You wanted it, you got it."

Bryce continued conversationally, "We now have a search warrant. Andrew Silva, I have some questions to ask concerning the murder of Inga Swenson and the burglaries—"

"*Murder*!" The young man's voice rose to a pitch, as though he'd missed the changes of puberty. "Jon never said—talk to him—I didn't—"

Bryce watched him attentively. Andy couldn't seem to arrive at a complete sentence so Bryce decided to help him along.

"This house is Jon Craig's. The paintings in it were stolen by you. Jon planned the burglaries, you did them. I've talked to Jon, you see." Not exactly an exaggeration, not precisely the truth. *We lie in order to reveal*. It was a saying he'd read in a book on writing. He didn't know if he'd learned the principle first as a cop or a writer. Andy was a young man Bryce didn't think capable of thinking ahead to the more complicated questions, like those of evidence in court. He would react to the moment. Bryce said, "On Halloween evening the painting leaning against the wall there in the dining room called *Lady at Tea* was taken from the Swenson home. We found Inga Swenson strangled in her kitchen not long after. I'm going to read you your rights—"

Andy's gymnastic shoe slid in the gravel at the bottom of the stairs but he recovered his balance and negotiated the turn around the van with the expertise of the ex-football linebacker he was. But Bryce jumped down the side of the stairs, cut across the front of the van, and threw himself against the door just as Andy, to hoist himself in, had got one hand on the door, one hand on the jam. So it was for his hands he screamed when Bryce's bulk hit, for the pain in those dangling fingers and lopsided wrists that his face screwed up in agony. Bryce withdrew the pressure, Andy slid to the ground.

"No way!" he screamed with combined pain and panic. "*No way*! I didn't kill her. And I can prove it—"

A group of deputies made their way to them out of the forest.

"—you're one of the witnesses. I was back at the party before she even left," he said between gasps. "And you saw me. I was the drummer in the band."

And, piercing through his elation, Bryce knew this to be true.

Hours later Bryce rang the doorbell of the Craig home and waited.

"It's been quiet," he had been told by a deputy. "He hasn't so much as peeked his head out the door."

So, without invitation, he walked cautiously through the house. The kitchen was swept antiseptically clean. In the dining room a breeze fluffed a curtain through an open window. The Halloween dummies gathered in one corner viewed him coquettishly through the waves of material. All the French doors in the lower rooms were open wide, draperies tied back tightly. The carpet was brushed straight up, as though freshly vacuumed. Much of the furniture had been moved to the other house. And, oddly enough, for a house once flamboyantly overcrowded these conditions served to dispense a sense of emptiness rather than space.

Climbing the stairs, he stopped to listen. It was quiet. At the landing he found the studio door open. He touched it lightly with his finger and it swung open wider, hinges squawking. Dried clay was all over the floor, the tables littered with black-ringed coffee cups—theirs from yesterday morning making him aware of just how distant yesterday had become. There was the plate of stale pastry by the sink, a stained smock on a hook. It was the only lived-in looking room in the house. Katharine's bedroom was more obviously abandoned: drawers hanging out of the dresser empty, bedclothes left in a pile on the bed, closets open and echoing.

The other rooms along the corridor had the impersonal air of motel rooms ready for the next visitor.

Jon's room was at the end of the hall. Bryce knocked,

soft but unmistakable. He tried the knob, it opened easily. Jon sat in a chair of throne-like proportions, as if there specially to receive him. There came a weak cry from the white cat he caressed on his lap.

"Shh. It's only Kevin," he told the cat. "Come in, Kevin. How are you?"

Bryce moved in slowly. "I've been busy."

"Ah, yes. Very busy, our Sergeant Bryce."

"We have Andrew Silva in custody. He was arrested at your house outside of Sierraville," he said, not willing to be disarmed or deterred, to have Jon divert the conversation to discussion of the weather. Jon's lips grew tight. Bryce thought he might refuse to speak at all. Jon ran a finger carefully down the cat's back.

"Beautiful cat," he said. "That moron of a vet wanted to put her to sleep but I wouldn't let him. She's a good cat. Had her fixed. Too bad I couldn't have done that to Katharine."

Bryce held his tongue, actually shoved it in the space behind his eyeteeth. It was a holding exercise like the one he practiced while waiting for the search warrant, to keep him from shoving his fist into Jon's mouth. Finally, he said, "I'm here about Andrew Silva."

Jon gazed at him with spinsterish disapproval.

"But that's not true, Kevin. After all, what's there to say? I plotted the burglaries and he carried them out and now he'll go to jail. He's a good boy, though. He can follow instructions well and that's what counts, isn't it? I like people intelligent enough to follow instructions."

"Especially when they acknowledge your intelligence as greater than theirs."

Jon missed the irony. "Of course."

"And Evan?"

Jon's nose twitched as if he'd caught wind of something unpleasantly pungent.

"I was going to be happy in that house—with Andy. I could have been happy here—with Katharine. But she wasn't willing. Katharine, as you know, has the morals of an alley cat. Hadn't even said a decent hello to everyone when she went running off with Evan that night. She had no business going to his house. There could be only one reason to go there alone. I don't care what she *says*. Experience proves otherwise.'' Jon stopped, breathing as though he'd been running and was trying to recover his breath. He started again, more composed. ''I did kill him. It was easy and it was practical, a completely sensible thing to do to achieve my goals. What *isn't* sensible is my tolerance of Katharine's behavior. She's a liar. She's lied to me and stay with her long enough and she'll lie to you, too. I know she got into my safe, you see.'' Jon was watching his hand delicately stroke the cat. ''She *pretends* indifference, but the moment she gets the chance she stabs me in the back. If you imagine she did it for you, you'll be sadly disillusioned.''

Bryce said, quietly and firmly, ''She didn't do it for me.''

Jon raised an eyebrow, a terrible parody of a gesture Katharine often made.

''You don't understand, do you? A woman who leaves her husband for another man will soon leave him for another.''

Bryce refused to be drawn in any further. ''The issue here isn't Katharine and her loyalties, but you and the burglaries. And Evan and Inga's murders.''

But Jon continued on as though, during this talk with Bryce, it had been an accident that they had touched on the same subjects at all.

''I tried to save her, to make her good. I was very ambitious. You see, it was up to me to make the family respectable after the scandal with her mother and father. You probably don't know about that—before your time, Kevin. So many years ago. But all that filth—all that—you couldn't walk down the street without people whispering. It was no atmosphere to bring up a young girl in. So I took it on myself to improve the situation. And did well,'' he said, earnestly, like a youngster tells himself a fairy-tale, until he can recite every word with conviction. ''And not only that responsibility, but others as well. People need guidance and discipline. Most aren't properly goal-orientated. But, like the biblical good shepherd, I made myself available to them. To atone—''

Bryce started to ask, *Atone for what*? But Jon seemed to have gone yet one step further over an emotional boundary. His face took on a childlike quality—sincere, innocent. A Victorian child, prim and proper and no-nonsense.

''—but I have atoned. I have been kind, listened to people's problems, helped them arrange their lives, though they don't properly appreciate me. I deserve my private house. It's a sanctuary for myself and for Andy. I have been *very* good but there is so much . . . I can't stand not achieving goals. I don't like the whispering. Yet, I've remained patient. I deserve all I can take.''

A child with a moral.

''Not like Katharine, not like her mother. Have you ever seen a picture of her mother? There's one over there by the bed,'' he said. But Bryce made no move to see. ''Beautiful, like the *Lady at Tea*. I loved her. But she was not . . . she betrayed my *ideals*.'' Jon leaned forward. ''She was with me that night she died. She came to me drunk, I sent her away drunk. She was drunk when she missed a turn and drove into the lake. I wasn't sorry. She said she wanted me to understand why she couldn't . . . but she certainly could with everyone else.'' Jon rubbed the cat's ears with more intensity. ''Katharine was so much like her when she was little, so spontaneous and affectionate. That's why I didn't want her spoiled. I wanted to bring her up in the way she should go; train her so she would be disciplined. But Katharine is hardheaded. There's something cold about her—''

And Bryce thought, Is it any wonder?

''She's grown less like her mother as she's gotten older. She was always a poor substitute. I could never make myself care in quite the same way I did for her mother. I actually prefer Andy's company. But I've failed him. I don't like failing, Kevin.''

The cat, upset by what she sensed in Jon, tried to get up and fell to the floor. Bryce could see she was stitched together, a cruel ragbag. She tried to arch her back and collapsed on the rug.

Bryce said gently, "Jon, you're going to have to come with me."

"Will I?" The child turned cunning. "When I was in your house I took more than that ridiculous Marin. I took seven of these." Jon opened his left hand. In it was a single piece of ammunition, a .357 magnum hollow point. Then with one quick, premeditated motion he took a gun from where it was lodged between the chair and cushion, stuck it in his mouth and pulled the trigger.

Thirty-one

Bryce wanted a drink. It was 10 p.m. and he sat in his half-lit office shuffling two messages. One had been left by Petter Swenson. He had just discovered that Inga had a flat tire in the trunk of her car, that the spare was on the right front wheel. As far as Petter could determine it must have happened the night of the party. He didn't know if this might be important or not.

Well, thought Bryce, neither do I.

The other was from Steve. He had arrived, safe and sound, and would be waiting in Tahoe City at that Pizza place on the water. Lakeview, he thought it was called.

Lakeview it was. Accurate, if unoriginal.

Bryce was going to ask Steve to stay with James rather than camp out on the couch, like he usually did. Bryce hadn't yet told Katharine about Jon and he didn't want Steve around when he did. For one of Katharine's strongest reactions, Bryce felt sure, would be relief. It was not an emotion Steve might be likely to understand immediately. A cold bitch, he had called her once. Bryce didn't expect her response to Jon's death to change his mind.

Bryce drove to the restaurant regretting the fact that he hadn't phoned Katharine. It was late now, and would be later still by the time he sat down and talked to Steve. He couldn't honestly tell himself he'd forgotten to call, and he wasn't trying to delay the inevitable—it was more complicated than that. There was a desire to protect mixed with guilt, a fear of what her own sound instinct might hear in his voice—even on a call just to say "I'll be late"—without his being able to see her face, without being within arm's reach. He couldn't stand the thought of the quietness on the other end of the line.

In the restaurant there was a scatter of customers, mainly locals. Some of them greeted him and he responded automatically. Cloistered in a far corner, away from the popular lakeview tables, were Steve and, perhaps not so surprisingly, James. They were drinking, heads bent over a set of stapled documents. On Bryce's approach, Steve got up and put his arms briefly around his father.

"What will you drink, Kevin?"

"Scotch. A double."

Steve grimaced. "I'll have another white wine," Steve told the waitress who had been hard on Bryce's heels. James raised a near empty bottle of beer and the waitress left to fetch the order.

"So," Steve said, when they were settled, "you think this sting is really going to work?"

"It doesn't have to."

James looked at Bryce with one eye.

Steve said, "Oh?" and looked surprised. "Did Jon make a complete confession?"

"In a manner of speaking."

"Great," Steve said heartily. "Then I can have a free weekend in Tahoe. He's in custody now?"

"He's dead."

"Oh," Steve said, as if he suddenly felt his good spirits out of place. He drank the last dregs of wine out of his glass. "Did he have an accomplice?"

"Yes. A young man."

"Is he dead, too?"

"He's in the hospital with a broken wrist and three broken fingers."

"Oh. Is that your handiwork?"

"The broken wrist and fingers are. Jon blew off the back of his head when I questioned him."

The waitress brought their drinks. Steve put his wine to one side and said, "Scotch, please. A double."

James seconded the motion but wasted none of the new

beer. Between large gulps, he asked, "Where's Kat? Has she been told?"

Bryce said, "Not yet;" and continued on evenly, "I don't think Jon killed Inga. And his accomplice was back at the party before she left. Petter left a message saying that Inga must have had a flat on the way home—there's one in the trunk and the spare's on the front."

"There's no way Inga could change a tire—she would have brought the whole car down on her head," James said.

"But," Steve asserted confidently, "if the murderer saw her by the side of the road, changed the tire for her, even offered to follow her home to be sure she made it safely and saw that he did so unobserved, it might be a perfect opportunity to commit his crime." He slid the set of documents in front of Bryce. "How on earth did you get that guy in personnel to copy this kind of information for you?"

Bryce smiled bleakly. "We have a lot in common. Besides old IOUs we both have ex-wives living in Orinda. It makes us kind to one another."

He started skimming the pages for the specifics that might give strength to his own bare-bones ideas.

. . . removed from family of origin at age twelve . . . Father described as volatile, alcoholic man who often hit his mother and intimidated the family . . . Mother projects an intense emotionality . . .

Steve leaned toward James and, apparently anxious to gossip, said, "I called Kevin very early this morning and heard a feminine sound in the background."

. . . Martin's verbal skills are appropriate and he has adequate social skills but his effect is generally bland and controlled. No evidence of a psychotic or major mental disorder . . .

James deliberately widened his eyes as if that were the most shocking thing he'd ever heard. "Kevin? I don't think he's—not in *years*."

. . . Interpersonal relationships have been chronically stressful and he tries to distance himself from close personal involvements . . . He generally feels inadequate but com-

pensates by setting high goals for himself . . .

"Well, something must have rekindled his interest. Do you think he practiced safe sex? As his son and heir do you think I should ask?"

. . . Generally capable of adequate impulse control and does not present an explosive or assaultive personality. However he normally overcontrols his feelings and impulses, but because he is subject to poor frustration tolerance and need for immediate gratification he can quickly become overstressed and, as a result, impulsive . . .

"Don't you know it's only those who can't do it themselves that are obsessed with the kinky details of everyone else, Steve?"

. . . Although he denies being sexually or physically abused, his test stories contain a marked victimization theme in which he is subject to feeling threatened by more dominant males. Consider this story which includes a rather mysterious reference to his father . . .

The waitress arrived with the Scotch.

"You want something to eat, Kevin? We already had a pizza."

Bryce looked up at the waitress. "Yes. Two burgers and chips—one order wrapped to go."

James eyed him curiously.

Steve wagged his eyebrows and said, "Who's number two for?"

But Bryce, at this point, did not feel inclined to answer that question. He said, "When I spoke to Russ in personnel yesterday he gave me some simple background information. I think it's possible that Martin Anderson is Inga's nephew. And his blood type matched the blood samples taken from Inga's home."

Steve possessed a precise and inquiring mind when it came to matters of finance. "Is he a beneficiary in her will?"

Bryce explained the terms.

"Well, you see? Sounds reasonable to me," Steve said.

But James shook his head. "I don't believe it."

"You're the one who suggested the idea in the first

place,'' Bryce pointed out tiredly.

''I said I thought he was sadistic, I didn't say he was stupid. If, by some odd chance, his father contacted him and told him about the will, wouldn't he also tell him Inga was going to die? Why kill her?''

Steve shrugged. ''Pressing financial needs.''

Bryce sat back to let them argue it out between themselves. He looked at his watch. Ten forty-five.

James reluctantly conceded the possibility. ''But what bothers me is that this guy was friendly with Inga. Inga liked him. He was becoming all but her social protégé.''

''Maybe he cultivated her on purpose.''

''Let's get acquainted so I can strangle you? You don't have to know someone in order to murder them. It makes more sense, in his case, if he doesn't associate with her.''

Steve's attitude was dismissive. ''Maybe his dad was an archetypical asshole—or had a weird sense of humor. He tantalizes the guy with stories about the will but doesn't tell him Inga is going to die.''

James' attitude was equally dismissive. ''If we tell the story—''

''This isn't a story, James.''

James blandly ignored Steve. Bryce checked his watch again.

''—start it with the assumption he knew that Inga was his aunt and even knew about the will, though I'm not sure that's an important point; we could say he was spurred originally by curiosity. Here's a young man from an ugly—more than ugly, a vicious background. Nothing but abuse from his father, a mother who mistook histrionics for caring. Even his face mistreats him, breaking out in pimples big as boils. And there wasn't much comfort in schoolfriends. This guy's got a severe social handicap—he's ugly. To overcome that would take a show of personality far beyond the confidence of our poor protagonist—''

''*Protagonist*? Jesus, James.''

''—but blind determination isn't beyond him. By working hard and disciplining himself carefully he gets himself accepted into a job that's more than a job—it's almost a subculture. People who still, in a way, manage to be on the outside and it's OK. He meets their requirements, though perhaps never his own. Does well most of the time, though sometimes his control cracks a bit under the pressure he puts on himself." James tilted back on the legs of his chair, thoughtful. "But one day, he gets lucky—he can hardly believe it. He puts in for a transfer to Tahoe and actually gets it. He's a good cop and Tahoe is happy to have him. So he comes out of hot, smoggy, dirty Los Angeles County into a cool lakeside community. Pine trees instead of skyscrapers, crisp uncluttered air, a friendly place intent on making tourists happy. A family place, in a lot of ways. Not a community where, one might add, it behooves you to act badassed—if you'll pardon the expression. He even experiences some culture shock.

"In addition he finds the flipside to his family life. Inga, apple-cheeked and kind. Petter, a prime example of Nordic manhood. He watches from a distance. Creeps close at odd social functions—the junior symphony, perhaps a place near them at the bar at Rosie's or Wolfdale's. He eavesdrops on their conversation, gets a better sense of who and what they are. Maybe he answers a 911 call at the ski lodge, meets Petter face to face. Slowly, not completely conscious of it, he's easing closer. Then, fourth of July, there's the picnic at the Tahoe Park beach enclosure. Inga and Petter are out on my boat, anchored right off the beach. This man is sharing steaks with another deputy and his wife. Into the water plops Inga's obnoxious little terrier. Since he's a cop, maybe it was a conditioned response, a kind of community-service instinct, to jump in and save the beast from the fifty-six degree water—to the sorrow of all but Inga. She thinks he's wonderful and takes a special interest in him—"

Steve leaned forward, listening seriously. Bryce glanced at his watch.

"However, he's never had this much positive attention before. On the one hand, it's nice. On the other . . . it makes him uncomfortable. He wonders if he deserves it. Worse still, he wonders what it would be like to get used to it, and, through some failure to live up to standard, lose it. Knowing the strained relationship between his father and his aunt, he might fear that discovering the family connection alone might be cause to sever their ties.'' James brought his chair down with a bang.

''Then comes the night of the party. Not everyone finds parties pleasurable. In fact, to this young man, parties bring back all the terror and anticipation he felt as an ugly and inarticulate adolescent. We're talking about a young man who views the most nominal social acceptance as a surprise, a source of suspicion. And then there's Inga, doing her best to make him feel comfortable . . .'' James trailed off as if losing the thread of his narrative, or perhaps stopping to search for the best words to evoke a happening both sensitive and subtle, one which they could not know the details of conclusively.

Steve was impatient. ''Well?''

Bryce said, ''What James is saying is that money is safer than love.''

''So he killed her to get her money. Isn't that what I said?''

''I think James' point is even if there'd been no money involved it might have happened. Anderson is afraid of people, perhaps especially of a family member, getting close to him. The Halloween party strained his already taut self-control. And Inga's niceness only made it worse. He didn't feel he deserved it, thought his appearance, his conversation, even his manners subject to criticism. He probably goes through an intense self-examination after every social encounter and never measures up. That's what I imagine he was doing when he spotted Inga by the road. It would be an automatic thing for him to make sure she made it home safely. But once she invited him in, God only knows what triggered his behavior.''

James interrupted distractedly, ''Remember when he attacked Claude? There was an attitude of revenge in that attack that interested me.''

Steve rolled his eyes again.

Bryce explained: "Anderson sees me with Claude, sees that Claude is anxious to talk to me, also observes that he is somehow referring to Petter. He knows I wanted to talk to him, that's why he was at the restaurant. It's quite possible that, panic-stricken, you might even go so far as to say paranoid, he thought Claude had information regarding the murder."

Ever practical, Steve said, "What now?"

"I should consult with the captain; the sheriff will no doubt need to become involved." Bryce sighed and looked at his watch.

"Why the *hell* do you keep looking at your watch? Do you have someplace else to go?"

Bryce responded smoothly, "I should probably consult with him tonight. Given Anderson's state of mind I think he'll break down under questioning pretty easily."

James was interrupting again: "I know you didn't want me to read that report, Kevin. I know it's none of my business. But you did use me and fair is fair. What was the part in the report about him feeling threatened by more dominant males—?"

Steve said, "Claude was definitely *not* a more dominant male."

Speaking kindly because his mind was on other things, James told him, "I wasn't thinking of Claude. Kevin, didn't you just suspend this panicky and unstable young man? And, pardon me for saying so, but aren't you in your own quiet way a more dominant male? And what happens when a person of his temperament becomes threatened or defensive?"

Steve took a tentative sip from his Scotch and wrinkled his nose. "That's a good point. But then again, if you say he's not stupid, what would be the point?"

"He's been suspended but that doesn't mean he couldn't have been listening in on the police band," Bryce said quietly. He and James were looking at one another in the peculiar way of people who know each other all too well.

Steve appeared to be feeling left out and slightly bewildered.

James asked, very gently, ''Kevin, where's Katharine?''

Bryce said, ''I need to make a phone call,'' and got up immediately to do so.

Steve threw up his hands.

Thirty-two

Katharine brought her work in, spread it out over the kitchen table and made feeble attempts to improve it. She had intended this piece to be a straightforward, even classical, work. A pair of hands—beautiful hands like Bryce's—on a woman's breasts. But as the shapes emerged it was clear it wouldn't turn out as she had imagined. The fingers were digging into flesh that was sure to escape. She frowned, annoyed, but feeling somehow it was better than her first conception. It confirmed her basic pessimism. She swore at it, felt better for having done so and then decided it had been silly to try to work the first day in a new place. She didn't usually. It was rushing things.

Hungry, she hunted from cupboard to cupboard, finally coming up with a half-empty bag of stale nacho tortilla chips. She ate, opening and closing cabinets methodically, as though playing detective.

She was still wondering about those stationery supplies, though she knew now the typewriter sat on the desk in the bedroom, that it even had a sheet of paper in it. She hadn't read what was on the paper. Very properly she hadn't taken the slightest glance. But she knew it was there, all right. A white sheet standing up from the roller straight as a signpost.

She wandered into the living room—in her opinion, a perversely masculine room. The colors were winter ones: gray and black wood and stone. There were no flowers, not even an empty vase anywhere, only books, a bottle of Scotch—Glenfiddich, with its elegantly rustic label—an old soda syphon, probably from the '30s, a cigar still in the cellophane. She stood by the fireplace where Bryce's empty glass from the night before still emitted a faintly brandyish air, mixing scents with the mustiness of the bear rug. The rug glared at her with glass eyes; she tweaked its snout with her toes. The brandy glass was the only thing he'd left lying around. (Her shoes lay in a heap on the floor, her keys spread out on the table, and she knew in the bedroom her clothes were strewn over a chest.) To wear his shirt she'd had to fetch it out of the laundry basket. He was, apparently, tidy. She didn't like that. And studying the room she realized it was one which invited no change, did not completely welcome her. It was as if she'd invaded a monastery.

Perhaps the masculine perversity lay in the fact that in spite of all this it still remained attractive.

She wondered what he did when he wasn't being a policeman. Something athletic, no doubt. Probably played basketball with the sheriff's team. No, he was too short for basketball. Golf? Oh no, don't let it be golf. Softball? Yes, softball with the team. And he was good at it, she was sure. She tried to imagine herself at a softball game. And failed. She squirmed at the thought of chitchat in the stand with other girlfriends and wives. *Wives*? That was another thing she couldn't imagine. Repeating the vows. If you didn't say anything you couldn't be proved a fool. And changing them seemed like cheating. But she took heart from the fact that marriage didn't seem to interest Bryce, and surely there were no softball games in winter. By summer she could be long gone.

But she wasn't ready to go yet. In a sense she wanted to see how far this man would let her go. She was confident he would find a way to get rid of her when it was time—she would be sensitive to it. In the meantime she liked sleeping with him. Perhaps somewhere in the back of her mind she'd been hoping once might rid herself of the desire; or that she might be disillusioned by the experience and therefore rendered safe. But, to put it simply, it hadn't worked that way.

She could get used to it.

But could she get used to him? What on earth would they

have in common other than bed?

She ran her foot through the coarse fur of the rug, glanced at the steep staircase. Throwing the empty chip bag in the fireplace, she climbed the stairs without hurry, sliding her hand up the cool pine banister. Closets were open, stocked with an assortment of flannel shirts, a few cotton Oxfords, Levis, one outdated suit and a tweed sports coat in lamentable condition. There were a couple of parkas, skis propped in the back and a pile of sweaters on a shelf overhead, none of them new. She took one, smelled it, tucked the rough wool under her chin for a few moments, thinking. Then put it back, still rubbing it.

She felt no guilt when she went to his desk. Because if he'd really minded she knew he would have put it somewhere out of sight, maybe even under lock and key. She rolled the cylinder.

Chapter Eleven. James' book. Bryce was working on the revisions. The chair creaked as she eased into it. A box with the rest of the manuscript sat next to the typewriter and she spent the rest of the day reading it with more careful attention than she had previously; laughing right out loud at some parts, sobered by others. She stayed there until she was forced to turn on the light against the growing dark, ignoring her need for more substantial nourishment. She curled her knees to her chest and sat for a long time after she'd finished, not thinking exactly, but rather the opposite—trying not to think. Until she heard the banging of the front door, saw the glow from a light switched on downstairs.

''Kevin?'' she called happily.

There was no answer. After a minute she got up.

''Kevin?''

Maybe something was wrong. She hadn't given Jon any thought today. Over the years she had given him more thought than he deserved. She felt sorry for Bryce. Takes a woman home and gets a shitload of family problems in return. She came down the stairs to find an empty living room, glanced out the window but saw only the MG. She approached the kitchen entry.

"Kevin?"

The first blow sent her reeling against the counter. And irrelevantly, through the pain, came the thought, *I'm getting tired of this*. This blow was a lot harder than Jon's, more direct. This man was one strong sonofabitch. She started to slide and he picked her up by the front of her shirt and slammed her against the cabinets. His face was set, so hard if she'd had a chisel she could have carved on it. She could feel her heart thudding against his knuckles, his shoulder holster pressed painfully into her ribs.

"I am going to kill you," Anderson said, deliberately pronouncing each word.

And Katharine, quite rightly, believed him.

Bryce let it ring five times, then beat the telephone once with a flat palm.

Sonafabitch!

He slammed down the receiver. Apprehension, unreasonable because there was no concrete evidence, yet not unreasonable because he could imagine the logic so well, pushed him through an oncoming crowd of college students, sent him running to his car.

James, sitting on the edge of his seat, saw Bryce pass by the doorway and said, "Jesus, God, no," and got up to chase after him.

And Steve, confused but unwilling to be left out, followed murmuring his own special blend of obscenities.

Anderson kept a hold on her shirt. But her feet were on solid ground, eyes looking straight into his. *I don't like being hit!* A simplistic thought overriding every other logical emotion; the one making her muscles taut, keeping her staring into the blue that were supposedly the mirrors of his soul. They were bloodshot. *You have no right*! she wanted to scream. But she could see if she opened her mouth he would slap it shut for her. That was what he was waiting for. A response. He was looking at her in a way not dissimilar from the way Jon would when he was watching for a loophole.

No way, bastard. You do the talking.

But Anderson was no great talker either, and it seemed they might keep this awkward standoff going until morning or until Bryce came home, whichever came first.

What came first was the telephone, screaming overhead.

They both flinched. Anderson held her close, looking as pleased as his stiff features would allow. "Answer it," he said and pushed her forward into the table where her work lay. Where, mixed with the odd bowls and tools of her trade, at a cursory glance looking like a transistor radio, the stun gun lay within an inch of her fingers. She felt his hand on her shoulder. She turned, taking the gun in hand, and with one fluid motion shoved it into his side and flicked the switch.

The element of surprise. For ten seconds, she had it. Around the table, into the living room. Do not pass go. Pick up the keys and run. Out the door. Across the yard. Still free. But God, he had to be coming—spin her around, throw her into the dirt in the next second. No, she was opening the car door, fumbling for the right key, felt exhilarated as it slipped into the ignition.

She heard the rapid succession of clicks associated with dead batteries, burnt out alternators, or starters given up the last ghost. Anderson was pulling open the door. How Jon would enjoy this, Katharine was thinking. It would satisfy his Victorian sense of justice. After all, it was his car.

They weren't quick enough. James and Steve were forced to maintain Bryce's erratic pace without the benefit of a glowing red ball in their window.

"Where's he going?" Steve asked.

James downshifted and swerved to the right to avoid ramming up the rear of a tired-looking VW bug full of students. They gave him a chorus of rude gestures barely discernible in the dark. Steve clutched the Alfa Romeo's dashboard.

"Home, I think."

"What's *home*?"

James turned in front of a fast moving BMW which skidded into the shoulder, out of the way.

"The woman you heard in his bed this morning."

"Who the hell—?"

"Katharine Craig."

"Oh, no . . . don't tell me. Shit," Steve said crossly. "When I told him she could stand a lot of watching I had no idea he would examine her so thoroughly."

On the traffic-free west shore Bryce took the lamp out of his window.

I can't hurt you.

It had been a stupid thing to say, Bryce thought. And she'd seen through it in a second. She may have been untouched but she wasn't naïve. Just cautious. What made her choose him at that particular moment to be her first lover he did not completely understand. What did he know of the reasons for any of her actions? He could surmise the worst, hope for the best, but it was all guesswork. There was too much he didn't know. The one thing of which he was certain was that getting involved with her had been an unprofessional move that Anderson, with his own career shot to hell, could easily exploit to take Bryce down with him. Misery loves company. Except it wouldn't be just Bryce. Katharine could be the one paying for his mistakes.

Bryce pushed his foot down on the accelerator.

That is, if she hadn't already.

Pinned back with one hand, her wrists had gone numb. His knees sunk into the inside of her thighs while the gun pinched up and down the side of her bare waist as easy as a butcher trimming fat from a steak.

"You should be careful what you use on an intruder, ma'am. He may turn around and use it on you. That's why some people shouldn't have guns."

When she was a child Jon used to get her on the ground and tickle her until she cried. But she'd learned to steel herself against it, and now she wasn't ticklish anymore. If she could only find that switch in the back of her mind, cut off the creepy sensation of the electric shock twisting her skin around. She gritted her teeth, stared up at him with determination she didn't know she had in her. But he'd already switched off the gun.

He had her on the rug, her shirt pulled up just enough to expose her waist and stomach. He looked at her for a moment, as if puzzled. Then shoved the gun in her belly and let the trigger go one last time.

But she knew the sensation now, and was prepared for it. He stopped and she lay under him without struggling. The gun's case was plastic and with three heavy blows against the stone fireplace he was able to break it apart. She watched, but it wasn't really him she was seeing. She was looking for loopholes of her own.

He took a minute, thinking. Then bent down and kissed her. But Katharine kissed back using everything the past two days had to teach her. His head snapped back and for a brief instant she saw the whites of his eyes.

Oh, I know you, you bastard!

He was looking for a way to scare her, something for her to struggle against. And she'd be damned before she'd give it to him.

He brought her up, twisting her arm painfully behind her back, sitting her down on the couch with one final yank before he let go. She rubbed her wrist. The bandage on that hand was spotting red over the cut. She looked up at the six feet five inches she needed to reduce to size and said, softly, "You like doing that don't you?"

He squinted at her. She was moving her wrists, studying the motion, speaking as soothingly as if she were talking to a child.

"Hurting me. That's your method, isn't it? Against what disturbs you. We all have some kind of method. Some people use sarcasm, some use pen and paper, some use clay. And some people just beat the shit out of things. Control, that's what I'm talking about. Makes you feel good." She touched her jawbone with a finger. "Go ahead. Right there. Now."

He called her bluff. Out of one eye she saw stars. He had a hand as big as a catcher's mitt. She shook her head. "That's it. You got it right that time, Deputy. Never had anything quite like that before." She smiled out of the one functioning side of her mouth, got slowly to her feet. "I think I prefer the stomach to the face. But I guess my preference doesn't matter. It's whatever you like, isn't it?"

"You're full of shit," he said, but he was moving away from her to stand by the window. She knew better than to show relief, he could see her reflection in the glass. She moved to the fireplace, laid her head against the cool stone, let a finger follow the rugged line of mortar.

He said, "Your husband blew off the back of his head today while your boyfriend stood and watched."

The game of words was on. She shrugged. "Too bad."

Still watching her reflection, he said, "What's your method?"

She raised one smarting eyebrow. "I just go along for the ride."

"I guess you do. You're good-looking enough to get by with it." She stifled a sense of surprise. He moved to the other side of the window, perhaps dissatisfied with the view. "You and the sergeant should learn to close the curtains in the bedroom."

Her finger stopped. She said, "Why are you here? You don't want me."

"No, ma'am. I want the sergeant." There was an extra edge in his voice, a sudden excitement. Out the window Katharine saw a light flickering through the trees. *Keep him talking, girl.*

"You said you were going to kill me. If you want the sergeant, why kill me instead of him?"

In two long steps he had her by the hair, pulling her to

the window. She bit the inside of her mouth rather than scream.

"If that car passes that last house the only place it could be going is here. And it will have to be the sergeant, won't it? And he's going to walk in and find his lady all nice and freshly slaughtered."

And just then, the light went out.

Bryce hit a rock. He felt the steering wheel shimmy, the car swerve and threaten to go out of control before he brought it to a halt on the front lawn of his nearest neighbor. He got out, did nothing but give a cursory glance at the gashed front tire.

Cutting through the trees would be quicker anyway.

He let go of her hair and she eased back over to the fireplace.

"I'm not his lady, Deputy. I'm just someone you found in his bed."

He was smiling bitterly. "That may be, ma'am. But you're the wife of a man he just let swallow a bullet. It will fuck him up real good to find you dead in his living room, if you'll pardon the French."

Though she didn't especially want to know she asked, "Why do you want to do this to him?"

Maybe he couldn't really explain, maybe he just didn't want to, or maybe he was just getting tired. He said, "I don't know."

"You don't *know*, Deputy. Don't you think it's something you better articulate?" She nearly choked. *Oh, Jon, you're one hell of an instructor*.

Anderson was looking at her. His own skin was as pasty as hers was bruised. "You're going to be dead in a few minutes, ma'am. Explanations don't matter then."

For a moment, as if forgetting her predicament, she said, "Never complain, never explain. As a policy, Deputy, I do believe I'm forced to agree."

* * *

Jesus Christ, she was smiling. For one half-mad second, Bryce thought she was chatting amiably with Inga's murderer. But then he saw her face change. Perhaps if he had seen terror there, he would have caught on quicker. As it was, he knew her well enough to break into a run.

She saw the lights before he did. Did Kevin have any idea Anderson was here? Probably not. She felt an odd sense of apology. If she hadn't stayed Bryce wouldn't be finding a body splattered in his little monastery here. The car paused, moved on rapidly. Anderson was watching it. Katharine was watching the fireplace tools. Shovel, broom, iron poker. If she took hold of that poker she better get him good because if he got it and started using it on her she was dead meat.

Ah, shit, she was dead meat anyway.

Anderson was reaching for his shoulder holster. She took the poker in both hands, wielding it like a baseball batter going for a home run. But Anderson was quick and strong and caught the blow at chest level before it could do the required damage. With both hands he pushed it back on Katharine until he had her wedged against the fireplace, gasping for air.

"Clever boy. He's still going to get the better of you."

One hand had enough strength to hold her, despite her struggling. The struggling seemed to give him extra energy. The other hand was pulling the gun from the holster. Katharine heard for the first and the last time: "Ma'am, you talk too damn much."

The window shattered. A second later the side of Anderson's head exploded before her eyes.

When she woke up, James was cleaning her face with a washcloth. Steve was taking a drink from a bottle of Scotch. And Bryce was speaking calmly into a hand-radio, words she couldn't understand.

Thirty-three

They moved into a resort, an empty one Petter had been trying to sell, and installed themselves in the manager's cabin. On Christmas Eve Bryce took her to a restaurant on the water and presented her with an envelope. In it was a card and a series of tickets. He would take her to San Francisco, they would stay at a small bed and breakfast off Union Street, this was what they would see: a ballet, an opera, a play, a football game (to broaden her education, he said), a cabaret show, and so on.

He had taken a lot of time selecting those tickets, wanting to please yet not exactly sure what would. Despite a reasonably contented surface he suspected an underlying restlessness, a feeling she was biding her time. He hoped a gift like this might ease the tension, might prove it was all his imagination.

And indeed, more than just pleased, she seemed genuinely excited. Even over the football tickets. He felt relieved, if not completely reassured. He was getting used to, if not fond of, the minefield of dirty clothes she left behind her, the trail of half-full mugs of cold tea.

But that night, as he sat in bed, she presented him with an envelope of her own. She strolled to the window, rather than join him under the covers, and stared out at the falling snow as if it were remarkable and new, though there was a six-foot snow pack covering the ground.

So it was with some trepidation that he opened the envelope. It contained a card and two airplane tickets. They were to Ireland.

"Why Ireland?" he asked.

"I gave James' globe a spin and that's where my finger came down."

She was lying. He nodded meaninglessly and gave more meticulous attention to his gift.

"Katharine," he ventured after some time. "These tickets are one way."

She moved her head up and down, once.

"That's not a mistake?"

She shook her head.

"I see," he said, though he didn't at all. "One question. If I don't use my ticket, are you going to use yours?"

She looked at him as if puzzled. Then laughed and managed to do it without being unkind. It could easily have been interpreted as a "yes" typical of an evasive personality, or the reluctant "no" of an embarrassed one.

And Bryce, at this point, didn't feel inclined to test it.